Run With the Hunted 7:
The Casino Job
By Jennifer R. Donohue

For Jim

Chapter One

When we are discussing a job, it is very rare for one of us to just outright say no; in fact, I'm not certain it has ever happened. There's all manner of back and forth about feasibility and approach, but when one of us brings a job to the table, we've always looked at it as a yes, if perhaps qualified. This time, Bits says no.

I am *extremely* surprised. I pause mid sentence, having just said "casino." Bits is frowning and blinking as though she is *very* alarmed and had perhaps only been half listening before I said that particular word.

Our new colleagues, Perry and Garnet have only done two very small, very easy jobs with us, and they look at each other uneasily, Perry laughing nervously. They stop when they see me looking.

I take a sip of sparkling water, refocus on Bits. "I'm sorry, darling, I hadn't finished speaking yet. Perhaps you can explain why you are saying no?"

"We aren't doing a casino job," she says. "Even a year ago, we wouldn't have." Her eyes dart briefly to Perry and Garnet but for a different reason than I looked at them. She eloquently, to me, means their lack of experience and lack of time with us.

Garnet takes it as entreaty for support, and looks between us. "Well why don't we hear Bristol out? Maybe we could do a casino job?" She smiles at me, seeking approval. Garnet is particularly disposed to my way of doing things, taking a social situation in hand and steering it in one's favor.

"If Bits says no..." Perry starts dubiously, then shrugs. "I don't know, casino jobs are a big deal, aren't they?"

"Yes. They are," Bits says, her eyes still too wide.

"Oh, I see, I've simply given the wrong impression! I don't mean a *traditional* casino job, darling, we won't be taking *their* money. Look at this exhibition! All of these art pieces covered in all of those diamonds." I pull out my phone, gauche in conversation, but I forward the exhibition announcement to Bits. "And the casino is right in town." Town being Paris.

"I thought we learned our diamonds lesson last time?" But her eyes are unfocused, looking at the information. Perry and Garnet exchange a look; they've heard about the diamonds job, of course, anybody in our sort of profession has heard scraps and whispers of it. It caused quite the ripple in the ecosystem, even though that was not our intent.

"We know how to handle them much better, yes. And can't you scout them, make sure that they are exactly what meets the eye? There are ever so many articles about the artist." I could put on a much more wheedling tone, but I'm certain Bits won't notice either way. Such nuance is not Bits's area of expertise, and it does not sway her. "Marquis is the one who told me about the exhibit, and who mentioned they might perhaps know at least one buyer who would like these items intact, thus we would not be handling the diamonds individually."

Bits is quiet for a long time, thinking I presume, or looking up that information. Then she says, "What's the play, then? How do you think we're going to go into the casino and take what isn't theirs but is very much covered under their security umbrella?"

"According to at least one article I've read, they place a protective cowl over each piece every night, and then shift them around, to create the illusion that they've moved when nobody is watching. Then other staff unveil them in the morning. They're all endangered or extinct species, so their movement is part of the lesson of the art."

"So you think that we'll insert, posed as the art staff, and instead of shuffling them around..."

"Shuffle them right off the floor to a waiting vehicle, yes." Perry perks up at that, but doesn't interrupt. They are very focused on vehicles, every aspect of vehicles. Operating, maintaining, enhancing. But Bits is quiet again, and though I have the unusual impulse to continue explaining myself, and pleading the case for this job, I wait. Bits has her own calculations to make, and is forever ferreting out information even as we speak. Garnet fidgets, looking at me, and picks up her drink instead. We are meeting at my flat, which is only one floor above street level, and the evening traffic outside of the window has already tapered off.

Will is occupying himself in the little library that we've built. I enjoy the library for the way all of the book spines are pleasing to the eye; he enjoys the library for the pleasure of selecting the books at the old booksellers that we go past on our walks, for taking in knowledge that he otherwise would not have found, for the escape that novels allow. He does not particularly care to involve himself in our criminal pursuits; indeed, they still seem to pain him. I've told him that there is no shame in stealing from rich people, who have earned nothing, but he isn't able to embrace that philosophy, despite the source of his chosen name. Perhaps one day. He's still becoming accustomed to this life, to his freedom.

"We aren't doing something like this without Dolly," Bits says finally.

"Without *Dolly*." In all of our association, Bits of all people has never caught me socially unawares. I ought to have expected this, though. There's been a Dolly shaped hole in our life these months now, nearly a year, and we simply do not address it. Perry's eyes widen; if Garnet is a bit of a baby duckling to me, Perry seems to have a near-worshipful regard for Dolly, though it is impossible to tell how they might have heard of Dolly in the first place. Our reputations precede us, always.

"If we're going to do something that even vaguely resembles a casino job, even if it isn't anything to do with the casino's own money, I want Dolly to be with us. We need her abilities and experience. So I guess it's a qualified no."

"It isn't as though you're asking for the *impossible*." I sip my water again, my last memories of Dolly coming to mind as though they'd been eager for the opportunity. Her bundling me into the car away from Will, me swearing I would never forgive her if she did exactly that. Slapping her in the face. And then her saying exactly the right thing to make sure I straightened myself up and returned to the party with my façade intact. That was it. I never even thanked her, once Will showed up at my side again two hours later. His façade is less unshakeable than mine, but I have also never been able to get him to tell me what happened.

"She hasn't been working," Bits says. Bits also never told me what happened.

"Perfect, I'll just go to...wherever she is, and whisk her away back to us." I am certain that simply calling her will not be appropriate, it must be in person.

"Hong Kong."

"Oh, is she there with Butler? Perhaps he can be entreated to join us as well." A range of emotions swiftly crosses Bits's face, so swiftly that I am not prepared to parse or interpret them. I spend so much time not needing to read her flat affect that it did not occur to me that I would have to be prepared to. This is indeed troublesome, or at the very least perplexing.

She shrugs. "Probably not."

"Hong Kong? Bristol, you're going alone?" Garnet asks, trying not to sound too eager, the sweet girl.

"I'm afraid that I will, darling, it will be simpler and swifter that way. I could travel professionally, were I to ever give the rest of this up."

"Did I hear Hong Kong?" Will asks, appearing in the doorway and pausing when he sees us gathered.

"Yes, darling, I'm going to take a quick little trip to see Dolly. You won't even notice that I'm gone."

"Of course I'll notice," he says, but he's got the shadow of a frown on his face. "Did she invite you? Does she know you're coming?"

"Well, I mean for it to be a surprise, but I'm certain Bits will do what she feels best in that regard. I give myself into her hands." I look from Will to Bits, who has a distinct 'arranging travel plans' look on her face. "I'll just be there and back again, no need to accompany me."

"If you say so." He seems about to say more, but crosses the room to the liquor cabinet instead. Dolly does put him on edge, the poor dear. "Is this to do with the job you're planning?"

"It is, yes."

He nods, mixing himself a gin and tonic. "Anybody else?" he asks the room. He knows that if I wanted a drink, I would not have the water.

"Yes, thank you," Garnet says. Perry shakes their head, and Bits almost never drinks alcohol and is not part of that equation. He hands Garnet the first drink he mixed, and pours another.

"I guess just let me know if you need me," he says, coming and brushing my cheek with a kiss.

"Of course I will, darling."

"You might want to get packed," Bits says. "I can get you on a flight in three hours."

Chapter Two

It is a long flight to Hong Kong, but first class makes it more than bearable. They have a very nice midrange champagne on offer, and when the flight attendant asks the occasion, I tell him that I'm on my way to reconnect with a friend. At the time, he smiles politely, and moves on to the other flyers.

Hours later, though, as we are disembarking at Hong Kong, that flight attendant approaches me while I wait and watch everybody else bottleneck as they try to rush off of the plane. "I hope that your time with your friend goes well," he says, and he hands me an airline branded tote bag.

"Thank you ever so much," I say, pleasantly surprised. He continues up the aisle, to help those passengers depart more easily. I peek into the bag to find a small bottle of that same champagne, with a ribbon tied around the neck, cushioned by airline neck towels and, judging from touch, a cold pack.

Once the way is clear, I disembark and take the airport train over to the vicinity of Dolly's address. Bit seems unsure that this will be a successful trip, but also did not try to dissuade me. After all, Dolly's inclusion was her stipulation. If I do not convince Dolly to join us for this job, there is no job. Or, there is no Bits. I could possibly find another hacker, but I'm not sure another one would work with me in those circumstances. Best to not worry about it for now; I cannot imagine a scenario in which Dolly does not say yes. I cannot imagine working with a hacker who is not Bits, or at least of her caliber, and how would I assess that in the window of time given?

Because I anticipated rain in Hong Kong, and barring rain, I anticipated drips from the air conditioning in Dolly's neighborhood, I wear a lightweight coat, and a hat, plain black from one angle, but when the light catches them, there are crystals sewn all over to make it look as though rain has fallen on the fabric. It's just the sort of subtle detail that delights me with its cleverness.

It is a bit late in the evening when I arrive at the address Bits provided me, but not so late that I think Dolly would be *asleep*, or even still eating dinner. I ring the bell and wait. Eventually, I hear the heavy tread of boots on stairs, and then Butler pulls the door open and looks at me for a little too long. "Why are you here?"

"I have a job opportunity to discuss." I don't allow my smile to waver, but his expression is one of studied blankness.

"She ain't here." He jerks his chin at the street. "She's fishing at one of the night places."

He won't be inviting me in, then. No matter. "It wasn't my intent to disturb you."

He gives a short laugh. "I'm sure it wasn't."

I look over my shoulder and back down the street, and turn back to Butler, my expression schooled into gentle entreaty. "There are more of those fishing establishments than one might expect."

"I'm sure Bits'll be able to tell you where she's at."

She would be able to, yes, but that isn't what I want. "I confess, Butler, this isn't quite the reception I'd anticipated."

"I'll bet it isn't." He sighs, stepping outside and shutting the door behind him. "It's the one with the animated sign, she likes how tacky it is."

"Thank you, darling, I appreciate your help." I start to turn, expecting him to walk me there, for why else would he have come out? Instead he lights a cigarette, planting his feet and looking at me as if he's making a decision, and I hesitate.

"I don't try to tell Dolly what not to do, that isn't how we work," he says thoughtfully. "But is there anything I can give you to just go away? Name a price."

"I...well, Butler, I really don't know what to say." I flutter a little to give myself time to take this in. I am at the disadvantage, not knowing what happened in the space between returning to my hotel and Will reappearing at the party. "I have a job opportunity, and we have been *such* a good team, it is very surprising to me that you would try to interfere with that. Would Dolly be happy, to hear that you said that to me?"

Butler takes a long drag on his cigarette, lets it out slowly. "I think you should look into fixin' your own heart, so that you stop being so careless with everybody else's."

I feel a flush spread across my cheekbones. "I beg your pardon, I did not come here to—"

"Nah, you came here to crook your finger and have Dolly come with you after whatever shiny thing caught your attention this time." He flicks ash off the end of his cigarette, perhaps giving me opportunity to protest. I remain silent; I will not bicker with him in the street. "You still got your secret agent man?"

"Will is doing well, yes." My ignorance notwithstanding, I did not expect this venom from Butler, which is I suppose my own fault. I *had* thought we were on congenial terms.

He nods. "Good. You get tired of him, don't leave him in a cardboard box by the highway, we'll come and get him."

"I'm dreadfully sorry that we were unable to be civil," I say, calmly, lightly. It is vanishingly rare for me to be caught so completely off guard. For it to be *Butler* of all people who has done so is extremely interesting. "I'll be on my way."

"You do that." He goes back inside, and for a brief moment, I stand looking at the closed door, waiting for Bits to comment on what just happened and make my feeling of...shock? Humiliation? She has the good grace to refrain. Perhaps she wasn't listening just now to begin with.

I'm certain Dolly's idea of tacky and mine are quite separate, but there is indeed only one fishing establishment along this thoroughfare with an animated sign. The fish is swimming through the stars when it sees something eye-catching, that absolutely enamors it, which of course turns out to be a fisherman's lure when he reels in his catch and holds it up triumphantly.

I walk through the entrance; an attendant sits behind a desk, flicking through an actual paper magazine. She takes one look at me and just waves me through without extracting the admissions charge. My heels are very loud in the tiled space and while the scent in the air is distinctly saline and fishy, it is somehow not unpleasant. After a long hallway, I come out to the fishing pool, a square room that is dimly bright. It is not readily apparent where the light comes from; there is some under the water itself, but not enough to account for all of it

The patrons sit in folding chairs here and there at the edge of the water. There are a few pairs, one larger group of five, all in suits, and more than one loner. Dolly is of course one of the loners, unless you count her robot dog as proper company, blinking its wide empty digital eyes at the doorway when I emerge. She's looking at the water, or seems to be, where her line hangs, but the dog's placement is obvious, even if her position of watchful repose is not familiar to the casual onlooker. She could be napping and still be able to tell you how many people were in the room.

As a result, I'm not surprised when she doesn't turn to greet me, and indeed waits until I've navigated the room and stand just behind her before she says, "Didn't know it was supposed to rain tonight."

"My experience here is limited, I simply assumed that it would." From what I can see, I am not standing close enough to be reflected in the water. "How—"

"Hyacinths," she says, still not looking at me. "There aren't extra chairs, unless you pay."

"I don't anticipate staying long." The bare mention of a chair does make me wish already that I'd gotten one.

"Right." She isn't being nearly as frigid as Butler was, but is a bit...wary?

I take a breath. "Dolly, before we say anything else, I want to apologize for striking you when last we spoke. It was a moment of extreme duress, and wildly inappropriate. I *do* hope you can forgive me, darling."

"You hope I can forgive you," she repeats, almost to herself. Then she turns partway in her chair to look at me, her arm over the back, fishing rod forgotten in her other hand for the moment. "You're unbelievable, you know that?"

"I've been told," I say, stiffly. I did not try to *plan* how the conversation with Dolly would go, I knew that would be a foolish endeavor. But this is also not how it works when I've apologized to somebody.

She laughs, and it's her usual too-loud, unaffected laugh, and that allows me to relax just slightly as it echoes off the tiles and the men in suits stop talking briefly, glancing our way. "Okay, yeah, you're forgiven for slapping me across the face in your 'moment of extreme duress.' I wasn't expectin' it, so you getting any shots in is on me, really."

Is it significant, to her, that she is actually deflecting the apology? Perhaps I am apologizing for the wrong thing. Or perhaps she has felt no need for apology. "It is rare to surprise you," I say. "For instance, you knew I was coming?"

"Practically heard you comin' up the street," she says. "But Bits said you got a job in mind, and asked if I wanted details from her or to wait for you. I said I'd wait for you. I expect she told you I was here?"

"No, Butler did."

Her eyebrows shoot up. "I'll bet that conversation was a real pleasure."

I hesitate a moment, and it is only part artifice. "He offered to pay me to go away."

She laughs again, genuinely delighted. "God, he's just perfect, ain't he?"

"I—"

"No, no, it's fine, you don't gotta answer that." She shakes her head, still laughing. "Go ahead, what's the job."

I take a moment to collect myself. I glance down at the robot dog, which has again settled itself, as though it is a real dog in repose at its owner's side. "There is an exhibition of diamond-encrusted statuary in a casino lobby," I say, and I pause for the 'no casinos' interruption that does not come. "They cover and move them every evening, after hours, and I think that would be our opportunity to take them to break them down and sell the diamonds. Or, sell the art pieces intact, if Marquis does indeed know a buyer."

"These ones're just normal diamonds this time?" she asks, ruefully, straightening out in her chair again.

I laugh on cue. "That I am aware of, yes."

"Casino job is a big deal."

"It isn't—"

"It's under their security umbrella. That makes it a casino job." That is straightforward reasoning that I cannot argue with, and rather than risk repeating myself to further plead my case, I wait while she thinks it over, making effort not to fidget. "You got other crew?"

"They're young and lack our experience, but yes. One who fancies herself my protegee, and the other who has been our vehicles specialist."

"How many jobs they got under their belts?" Her tone is one of clinical interest, she has not yet acquiesced. I am interested to find that I am not certain which she will decide. On the plane, I was certain. Then I spoke with Butler.

"Two, with Bits and I. Otherwise..." I trail off. I am aware that this is not in our favor. She mulls that over for a while longer, long enough that one of the couples packs up and leaves while I wait, coming past us with the studied gentle disregard for our existence that people who have long lived in close proximity affect. It's a social privacy measure, one that I appreciate.

Eventually, Dolly says, "Bristol, you know you don't have to keep doing this, right?"

"Pardon?"

"It ain't a secret that you like the fancy fun parts of these things, and winning, but not the gettin' shot at gettin' kidnapped parts of these things." I'm reminded, of course, of the morning at Rafe's where she coined the term sparkling abduction to try and make me laugh. I'm reminded of the relief, when she and Will got out of the car in Morocco. I'm reminded of playing the decoy, to draw Homeland's pursuit while she got herself and Bits to safety.

"One of those was—" She holds up a hand. Her left hand, I don't know if that is contrived or not, and it bothers me, a bit, to not know. Though also, so little of what Dolly does is contrived, I'm certain she wouldn't even think of it.

"No, I know, one was to save my skin, and Bitsy's, and I'll be thankful for that forever." She's quiet for another long while, watching fish come near her line, dart away again. "And you know I'll always come for you."

"I do know that," I say softly. It is necessary, I think, to drop all artifice for this moment. Dolly and I have always been unlikely friends, which I think has made the depth of our loyalty to one another that much more of a surprise to me. "There isn't a thank you in the world that would suffice for—"

"You don't need to say *thank you*." She stands up abruptly, her chair skittering back a few inches on the tiles. Her line makes a splash in the water, and from the look on her face, she'd forgotten it in that moment. She pauses, takes a breath, and reels it in. The robot dog gets to its feet and moves away just slightly, as though it sensed her change in mood and is giving her space.

"We *are* somewhat past thank yous, aren't we."

She makes a wordless noise that's very nearly a growl and folds her chair. "So Bits said hell no to the casino job and now you're here?"

"She said no the second that I said the word casino, and when I asked her to listen to my actual proposal, she did so, and then said that we would do no such thing without you."

She nods, studying my face. "So you got on a twelve or sixteen or twenty four hour flight to come and ask me in person? You want it that bad?"

"I—"

"No, that's not the right question. If I don't agree to do this, are you gonna do it anyway, without Bits and with the new kids?"

It is interesting to consider whether I think Bits wants Dolly to say yes or no. I indeed spent some of the flight meditating upon that. I pause just slightly, and say, "There are other hackers in the world."

"Fuck." I think, if Dolly wasn't holding a chair and a fishing rod, she would have thrown her hands into the air. The men in suits stop their conversation and regard us again. "Wait no, you can't fool me. Once you've had the best of something, you aren't gonna lower your standards, and Bits is the best we know of."

"That is very true, darling." I look at the people in suits, and Dolly looks over her shoulder at them too, and sighs.

"Come on." She walks away from the water and turns in her fishing pole and chair at the front desk. The girl looks at both of us with wide eyes, and I wonder if she's been watching us on whatever security they have here. Perhaps she's never seen Dolly so animated.

"Where are we going?" I ask once we're in the street.

"Well I gotta pack, right?" She picks up the robot dog.

"You're packing? You'll come with me back to Paris and do the job?" She's walking just slightly too fast, and I don't like having to rush to keep up.

"For your own sake, yeah, yes, goddammit. I'll come with you and do the job." She stops short and turns to me. "But listen, if at any point I think this thing is a no-go, you need to agree with me and drop it. I promise I won't pull the rug out from under you for meanness' sake, but I need you to agree to walk away if I say to pull the plug."

"Dolly, of course. I trust you utterly, you'll do everything in your power to do a job cleanly and with our best interests in mind."

"Jesus Christ," she says, meditatively, patting at her pockets with her free hand until she finds her ecigarette. "You ever get tired of your own bullshit?"

"Whatever do you mean?" She cuts her eyes to me and blows out a cloud of cupcake scented vapor.

Chapter Three

Dolly yells "Honey, I'm home!" as she clomps up the stairs, and I follow her more gingerly.

"Did you catch dinner?" Butler asks from the room above.

"No, but you'll never guess who I ran into."

"I don't have to guess, she came here first." We reach the top of the stairs, and Butler is smiling, looking at Dolly, and then looks past her at me and the smile fades. "And here she is again."

"Here she is," Dolly agrees, putting the robot dog down and going to give Butler a kiss. I have seen them together so rarely, and yet when I do, it becomes obvious that they complement one another well. Dolly had been both so forthcoming and also so guarded about her life and the people in it, that to have met Butler several times now feels almost as though it is a trick she is playing, a small inside joke that only they share. But also now I've met her parents, and other members of her family, and that sort of vulnerability and trust from Dolly is like being given a gift.

"Bristol, I'm sure you'll excuse us for a second," Butler says.

"Oh of course, darlings, take your time."

Dolly says "I'd offer you a beer, but—" and then Butler almost comically pulls her out of the room. Perhaps it is comically, she's laughing.

I'm left to stand alone in their living room, or main room; it's something of an open concept, with the kitchen adjacent, divided by a counter or island with stools at it. There are some digital frames on the walls, with carousels of photos rotating. One frame seems to be a fishing trip, ending with a marlin being displayed before returning to a photo of a docked boat. One is from the vantage of a helicopter, and having taken a flight in one of Butler's helicopters, that is almost familiar to me. And one is also on water and I only get a glimpse of the last picture before it rotates again to one of the ferries here. But there is something about the glimpse that I get of that picture that makes me wait for it to come around again, as the scenes flick through one by one, the city skyline, other passing boats, and then Butler and Dolly standing facing each other, with the ferry captain next to them and the crew gathered around, everybody smiling widely. I didn't mean to, but I reach out and touch the frame, stopping the rotation. Butler and Dolly facing each other, holding each other's hands. The ferry captain.

A door opens behinds me, and Dolly comes back into the room, Butler not far behind her. I turn to them, my fingertips still on the frame. "You've gotten *married*?"

Dolly had been speaking and closes her mouth, looking surprised, then grins. "Oh yeah, I knew I forgot to tell you something."

Butler laughs, finally. "Yeah it was an intimate ceremony," he says in a dry tone.

"That's so wonderful, congratulations to you both." I take three swift steps to close the distance between us and hug Dolly, and she stiffens with surprise and then sort of pats my back. I release her and look at Butler, and think better of that particular maneuver. I instead reach into the airline tote bag still hanging from my elbow and produce the champagne bottle. "I have just the thing!"

Dolly takes it, looking at the label. "Bristles comin' through with the good stuff." Butler snorts, but goes to the kitchen and retrieves glasses from one of the cabinets.

"Please, tell me everything," I say, as Dolly untwists the wire cage from the cork and works at it with her thumbs.

"Well geeze, he's proposed I don't know how many times over the years, but—"

"Just three," Butler says. "And you asked the first time."

"Okay yeah, so we've been idiots for a while now." The cork pops and Butler catches the initial foam in a glass, and then Dolly pours for all three of us. They aren't champagne flutes, of course, but one must make do. Butler hands me a glass, and then we three clink our glasses together. "But anyway, this last time, he got me right after I'd lost some blood so I was real vulnerable." She is grinning up at him and I can't help but search her visible skin for new scars; she is wearing a tank top and surplus pants, untied boots mais oui, and I do note a pale spot in her right shoulder, almost star-shaped.

"You had transfusions by then, I'm not a creep."

"Nah, nobody's accusing you of bein' a creep." She's got a little bit of foam on her upper lip, and he reaches over and wipes it off. "Thanks."

"Don't mention it."

I'm so delighted by the domestic scene, by the joy of the unexpected wedding, that I have been quite thoroughly side-tracked. Who would ever have thought that I would come here and find *Dolly* experiencing marital bliss? Other than Bits, apparently, that wicked girl. She might have told me; I would have bought a better present than a free bottle of champagne I'd just received. "Are you going to have another wedding?"

Dolly quirks her eyebrows at me. "What?"

"A larger one, with other people invited?"

"No, why would we." Dolly finishes her champagne. "Anyway, let me toss some stuff in a carryon."

She disappears back into that other room, leaving Butler and I looking at each other. "You're certain I can't convince you?" I ask him.

"Oh yeah, real sure. But she better come back in one piece, or I'm gonna be far less nice about it."

"Butler, no threatening Bristol," Dolly calls from the other room.

"Is that a rule now?" he asks, loudly enough for her to hear, but she does not deign to answer.

I smile, and I finish my champagne. This level of banter is more what I've come to expect. Even though what we are doing is sometimes deadly serious, there is only so seriously that I expect the participants to behave, which perhaps does not make sense. No matter. "My intent is for nobody to lose any blood over this." I was not aware of any blood lost last time. I cannot try to internalize that right now.

"My impression is that you always do your best to keep your blood on the inside." Butler collects the glasses and sets them in the sink.

"That isn't incorrect," I say, cautiously, curiously. "I think that is how most people function?"

"What, now you're calling us the freaks?" Dolly asks, reappearing.

"I was not—"

"Joking, it's okay." She looks around as if she is taking care not to forget anything. "I guess we *are* the freaks, actually. Free range former super soldiers, with varying levels of cybernetics."

"Sure," Butler says, affably enough. "And at least one of us still has both our natural born arms."

"C'mon, most people can't even tell which one's my fake one," she says, giving me a wink. "Ambidexterity and big chunk o' that misbegotten diamonds money saw to that."

"She's made a big deal her whole life about how she's ambidextrous," Butler says to me. "She can write on paper with both hands at the same time. Or could."

"Still can. You're just jealous."

"Yup, that's it." He reaches out and pulls her close, wrapping his arms around her. I never think of Dolly as a *small* woman, she very much is not, but Butler is a very imposing man. He rests his chin on her head a moment, and I have the very rare feeling like I am intruding, and I turn elsewhere, to give them the moment.

I suppose Dolly is like a cat and can only be held for so long, because she clears her throat and when I turn back, they're a step apart again. "You about ready? When's our flight?"

"Bits was taking care of that, I'm certain she gave us enough turnaround for a meal and to return to the airport." It is possible that Bits is sleeping, she *does* do that, I'm very certain. Not nearly enough, but she sleeps.

//You have a few hours,// Bits says. //Which unfortunately means you have enough time to hurry up and check in at the airport and then wait.//

"Par for the course," Dolly says. Butler looks at me.

"I want to make sure you're paying attention," he says, and I arch a brow at him, just slightly. "If you let her get hurt like that again, there will be hell to pay."

"Butler, you don't get to—" He holds up a hand and Dolly stops, looking amused but perhaps a bit frustrated. Dolly most certainly does not need anybody to defend her.

"I know. And normally I wouldn't. But I need Bristol to understand—"

"I have no intentions of letting Dolly get hurt at all," I say, looking from him to her. "It is never my intention."

"Cuts into profits," Dolly says lightly, reaching up to turn his chin so she can kiss him again. "Okay, we're outta here. I love you, I'll tell you when we get there. Or I'll text you from the airport until you get tired of me and tell me to leave you alone."

"I'll never get tired of you," he says with utter seriousness.

"Sounds like a challenge to me." She grins, and he laughs.

"Now get outta here before I keep you all to myself." They both laugh at that and then Dolly's hustling me out the door and down the stairs, her carryon bag slapping against her hip.

Chapter Four

We are such a disparate pair that the flight attendants on our flight to Paris don't even realize that we are flying together, which is amusing. Dolly is not the kind of flier they typically see in first class, and her grinning charm confuses them until they leave her alone and she cat naps while I catch up on all of the social gossip aggregates. Nothing important has transpired, it rarely does, but it's good to be informed should I be called upon to make that sort of small talk.

//How was it?// Will asks me at some point; he must have just woken up and wanted to check in.

//Fine, darling, we're on our way back.// Do I want to dwell on Butler's hostility? Not particularly. He's understandably protective of Dolly, while also wisely understanding that he cannot limit her actions.

//That easy?//

//Why wouldn't it have been?// I message back, and in the pause, I can see him starting to message, stop, start again, stop.

//I guess I shouldn't have doubted you,// he finally says. //Do you want me to meet you at the airport?//

//That isn't necessary, darling, we'll take a car.// If I was returning on my own, I'd have him meet me. With Dolly, I think that a car would be better, to prevent her from taking over the vehicle situation immediately and being able to detach from me socially. //Perhaps if you'll have lunch ready? You can call down the street for us.//

//I can do that.//

//Thank you.// I sneak a look at Dolly, who looks like she's dozing, but I know can be instantly alert from this position. I'm not certain I've ever caught Dolly actually sleeping. I feel so deliciously excited about this, to have our trio together in a room again, planning a fun little job. I hadn't allowed myself to dwell upon missing Dolly; we do bicker so, but it's all in good fun. It's simply how we best communicate, no matter what it must look like from the outside.

Neither of us checked luggage, and so it's a simple thing to disembark and walk out to our car. It isn't usual for me to travel so light, and I do change into a capsule dress and freshen up my hair and makeup while still on the plane, but this was not a trip with any sort of pause. If I hadn't myself gotten so accustomed to sleeping on planes, I would feel very dreadful indeed.

I did not give instructions for them to be present, but of course Bits, Perry, and Garnet are at the flat when Dolly and I arrive. Will, bless him, is doing his best to entertain them, and Garnet is doing her best to bat her eyes at him unsuccessfully, while Perry and Bits are instead talking about scooters or traffic cameras or some such.

"I hope you haven't been waiting long," I say, as Will comes and takes my bag, giving me a kiss on the cheek. I see Dolly note the kiss, even as she drops her bag on a chair by the door and takes in the room at a glance. I should ask her, sometime, what she sees when she does that. The exits, I'm certain, possible threats, I don't know what beyond that.

"No, we've only been here like twenty minutes," Perry says, looking at Dolly from the corner of their eyes, but determined not to be starstruck, I think. It is so very interesting to see a person meet their hero. "I'm Perry," they say, bulling on and making themself look directly at Dolly, who slaps on a grin and holds out her hand.

"I'm Dolly, I'm sure none of what Bristol just did is a surprise, though." Perry laughs, surprised, and Dolly laughs too, offers her hand to Garnet, who has a look of appraisal on her face that is not nearly as hidden as she might think.

"I'm Garnet, pleased to meet you."

"I'll bet. This is a hell of a job, I wouldn't want to do it without me either." She laughs again, making it all right for everybody to laugh. The manner in which Dolly can command a room is certainly unexpected; I've never given her credit for that. "Bitsy, I hear you requested me special."

"Of course I did," Bits says, blinking. "There's no way we're doing a casino job without you."

"It isn't technically—" I start, and Dolly waves her hands at me.

"Technicalities, schmechnicalities. It's in a casino, it's a casino job."

"Does that mean it was a casino job when we extracted Will?" I ask.

"Good question, actually. We started at one casino, and drove all over hell and damnation, but ended at a casino. Huh."

She shrugs affably. "Okay we'll work on the taxonomy." Will hovers in the doorway to the room, having heard his name, but unsure if he is wanted. "Is he involved?" Dolly asks.

"We had not gotten nearly so far as that in planning," I say, looking at his face. It's carefully neutral, but his eyes are slightly wide. He does tend to have that look about him when dealing with Dolly, though. "Darling, will you consider involving yourself with our little event?"

"It might be better if I was just in a support role," he says, perhaps trying to calculate the ramifications of his status as no longer technically alive in the eyes of the United States government, though we did procure a pricy new identity for him once we entrenched in Paris. Perhaps trying to calculate whether he wants to undermine our operation and get us all caught and then clear his good name, though I'm not certain how successful that would be for him. He is so *earnest*, though, I can see him making that mistake. It would be a shame to lose him so soon.

"In for a penny, in for a pound," Dolly says. "If you already know as much that this is a Casino job, you can implicate us anyway, so you might as well go whole hog."

"Oh don't say whole hog, Dolly darling, it sounds so vulgar."

"I mean, it is." Perry laughs and then looks slightly embarrassed. "Alright, Bits, you think this is doable? Is it really as simple as Bristles wants me to believe?"

"I think it could be, yeah. They don't seem to give the people dealing with the art installation that much oversight, since they have the security badges and things to be inside. They show up every night in the same van, wearing the same jump-suits, etc. etc."

"But is it the same people every time? That could screw us."

"No, it's been different people a lot. Something about ran-domizing the process so that the art is more natural or organic or whatever."

"Sounds like they want it to be spooky as shit," Dolly says, investigating the liquor cabinet.

"I believe the notion is for it to be playful," I say.

"Right, right, like they're live, diamond-encrusted animals frolicking in a meadow when you're not lookin' at them, sure." She turns away from the liquor without pouring anything. "Okay, so what are the roles here? We're not all gonna jumpsuit up and shuffle some animals and drive away?"

"Our planning process stalled when it became necessary to go and retrieve you," I say, smiling, and Dolly looks from me, to Bits, who nods, and then the rest of the room.

"Well okay, here I am. I assume I'm one of the jumpsuit wearing, drive away-ers, maybe Perry there too, and I guess Bits though that wouldn't be the best use of her talents."

"Bits would be best utilized in one of the vans, making sure the surveillance and other electronic concerns are well in hand," I agree. "And thus here is where Will could really be very helpful indeed."

"I could," he says, at an attempt to be game, the poor dar-ling.

"So that leaves you and Garnet."

"There are parts of the casino that function all night, and we would be well-positioned there, that we might cause a diver-sion should it become necessary."

"Meaning you already got your dress picked out," Dolly says.

"I may," I say. I do not, but in Paris of all places, forethought is not necessarily a requirement.

Garnet looks a little surprised, not quite panicked. "Oh, I don't though! I didn't have a clue that we—"

"You didn't need to have a clue, if anybody's on top of who needs what kinda dresses when, it's Bristol," Dolly says. "She's got all kinds herself, and lots of sources otherwise. And materials." For no particular reason, I look over at Bits as Dolly mentions materials, and she has the strangest look on her face.

"Bits, darling, what is it?" I ask, quite startled.

"Just thinking of spray can dresses," she says after a pause.

"They're so *interesting*, aren't they," I say, almost automatically. Spray can dresses might be as fascinating to me as those vending machine capsule dresses, the quality of wear that you can get out of both is shockingly similar, and I don't think that enough people mention them at all. Of course, the design of the dress itself when you're using the spray can is up to you, but the people who *engineered* them are simply phenomenal, they've gotten better even since the one that I wore in Morocco. Then I think of my missing cans from my room in Morocco and look from Bits to Dolly. "You'll forgive me for asking, Bits, but what has your experience been with spray can dresses exactly?"

Her eyes flick to Dolly briefly, and I do regret that I can't see both of their faces at once, but I can only imagine Dolly's expression will be fairly impassive. "At your hotel?" she says, like it's an obvious answer and confusing that I'm asking. I suppose it is.

I confess, I'm still trying to formulate an answer, or my next question, when Dolly tosses back her drink and says "Welp, it's getting late, I might as well head to *my* hotel."

"But everybody is here now," Perry bursts out, disappointment writ large on their face.

"That's very true, and though Bits is bangup at makin' sure surveillance doesn't know things like that, nobody's perfect. So the next time we meet it can't be at Bristol's I'm sure well known by now apartment or flat or mansion whatever they call this in Paris. Bitsy, you got any safe houses around here?"

"You'd be disappointed if I didn't," she says.

"Dolly, don't be ridiculous, you can stay here," I say finally.

"Sure, but we get in each other's way, and I'm sure we'll be close enough by the time it's game day. Plus, I want to call my husband and I want privacy for that." She winks, and grins, and Will clears his throat.

"Do you want to borrow a car?" he asks.

"Nah, public transit is fine while I'm getting my sea legs. It's been a while since I've been in Paris."

"You're going to go on the metro with your luggage? Really, Dolly darling, it's no trouble."

"I know it ain't," she says evenly, and I sigh.

"Suit yourself, you always do what you'd like anyway."

She laughs. "Oh, do I?"

"Yes, you do."

"Bristol, I'm sorry to interrupt, but I just remembered that I agreed to plans tonight," Will says apologetically.

"Plans? With whom?" I ask, and I'm surprised at the effort it takes me not to snap.

"The couple that Marquis introduced us to at that last gallery opening? The husband messaged me about a wine and cheese thing, said that his wife thought that he should have more friends and that I might be a good influence." This is very opportune, but also Will is absolutely terrible at lying, so he cannot have concocted this in the spur of the moment, to make way for Dolly's departure.

"Well I wish you had told me," I say.

"I thought I put it in the calendar, but maybe I forgot to sync them." He looks at Bits, who looks off for a second, and then gives a little nod, and my phone pings. I pull up the notification, and there is an engagement this evening with that couple, the Mornays, that was initiated weeks ago.

"I suppose that's that, then," I say, turning my smile to the room. Garnet has waited pensively, watching all of this interplay. Meanwhile, Perry is making every effort to not just have their gaze locked on Dolly at all times. "We will convene again tomorrow, perhaps? In a location that Bits and Dolly deem more secure than this?"

"You know how important opsec is, Bristles," Dolly says, picking up her bag again. Bits stands beside her; Bits hardly removes her jacket when she is here, preferring to slouch inside of it, replete with her electronic accoutrement.

"I could give you a ride," Perry say shyly, as everybody is making their way towards the door.

"Oh, you know, maybe you should. Sort of a trial by fire. Does that meet with your approval, Bristol?" Dolly tosses over her shoulder.

"It does, yes, it would be lovely if we could all become familiar with each other."

Garnet checks her watch; she got a lovely vintage piece from the open market one morning a few months back, still keeping accurate time, and has been very proud of it. "I've also got a date, actually," she says. "But, tomorrow!" She slips out the door before Dolly and is down the stairs in a wink.

"She normally skittish?" Dolly asks.

"Not really," Bits shrugs. "Excited about this guy, I think. He's in finance or something."

"Ooh finance," Dolly says, deadpan, as I shudder.

"Oh, finance," and we laugh.

Dolly looks at me, and Will. "Okay, it is good to see you, you know that, right? We'll get this thing planned. Go enjoy your snooty people party with your—"

"Oh darling please don't say one of your awful things," I plead theatrically.

"What would the cheese one be? Car shootery?" She grins and I shudder again. "Will, you take care."

"I try," he says, and then everybody else is out the door and he and I are left alone. "Did that go...well?" he asks.

"It didn't go poorly," I say carefully. I'm thinking of what I might want to wear to a 'wine and cheese thing' and pull up the event information to see where it is being held. I find myself looking towards the door occasionally, as if Dolly might reappear because she forgot something, or forgot to say something, or will stay here after all. But the door doesn't open.

Chapter Five

B its's safehouses are interesting places, ranging from the shipping container that we stayed in during our first diamonds escapade, to an old abandoned-looking warehouse or perhaps factory by the trainyards. It hadn't even occurred to me that a section of Paris might *look* so industrial and desolate, and yet here we are. We arrive staggered, of course, but I'm not certain I see a single person on our way. Will seems a bit nervous, but whether that is because of his reluctance to actually take the steps to *criminally* embroil himself with us versus just socially, or his persistent nervousness around Dolly, or something else entirely, I really couldn't say. He is, overall, a very steady and reliable man, and I don't doubt that he will be able to handle whatever it is that we run into.

The doors lock and unlock manually. I've asked Bits before why she does not rely upon biometric or smart locks, since she is so technologically inclined, and her answer was that it was because she was so technologically inclined that she avoids smart locks and biometrics at all costs, because they introduce catastrophic vulnerabilities, which was very surprising for me to hear, since they're so widespread.

"I've never done anything like this," Will mutters, and I reach out and squeeze his arm.

"You don't have to," I say, sympathetically.

"No, I don't. But I...well I'm a part of your life now and I'm not really comfortable as just a kept man either so we'll see how it goes," he says gamely. I can imagine him saying anything like that to Dolly, and how she would laugh and send him home.

"That's the spirit, darling," I say, and the door opens. Bits blinks at us like it's very bright outside, and I don't think it is, but she does prefer a cavelike atmosphere.

"You're the last ones," she says. "Dolly brought lunch."

"How very sweet of her," I say, wondering what made her choose to do so, and also wondering what she might have gotten, for a group with such disparate tastes.

Bits doesn't answer, just leads us down an industrial hallway, everything gray concrete or painted gray, wires and tubes and such running along the walls. Whether they're from the previous use of the building or whether Bits has them currently in use, I could not say.

We reach a large room, a table and chairs set up and seeming comically small in the expanse. I look up, and the ceiling is very far above us, and does have glass skylights that are covered in some manner. Not papered over, light still comes through, but there is almost certainly something technological going on so that a passing drone could not simply take in our business at its leisure, I trust Bits to have thought of that.

Perry is telling Dolly some braggy story, I can just tell from their posture, and Dolly is letting them, tolerant, amused. Garnet is sitting primly at the table, still wearing her coat, a silver can of sparkling water in front of her. There are paper bags on another table, I presume containing said lunch.

"So sorry to have kept you waiting, darlings," I say, dropping my purse on the table and shrugging out of my coat, which Will takes from me and then looks around before draping it on an empty chair. It is a bit chilly in here, I might want that back, but not immediately. "I was worried we would get lost on the way, but we've made it after all."

"I build it into the schedule," Bits says, which makes me laugh.

"How thoughtful of you, darling, thank you! Also, Dolly, Bits says you've gotten us lunch?"

"Ah, yeah, I passed a shop that had stuff in the windows that looked so good, I had to stop. It's funny that they still do that here, isn't it? Real actual stuff in the window, not a screen or an AR display or anything."

"Paris and Hong Kong are quite different," I say. Paris has passed ever so many restrictions regarding screens and displays and such out on the street. Being here is sometimes like being in an old movie, until you walk inside a building and it's the future again. One of the smallest fashion houses that also maintains a storefront has a device that you can step into in order to have your body scanned, and anybody who makes custom garments can use those to make your items to order.

"Yeah but are they? No, don't answer that. Are you hungry? I figured it was like lunchtime, we'd wanna eat, but you know me, I always wanna eat."

"I could eat," Perry says gamely.

"That's two. Come on, Bits, you're wastin' away. And there's no telling what Bristol and Will have already been up to."

"I'm sure I could find something to pick at," I say, glancing at Will, who nods. He is of course unused to the vagaries of

Dolly's generosities, passing a store of one type or another and gathering an assortment of items that she thought we might like. It's interesting, how accurate she is; one would not expect her to pay that sort of attention.

We get settled around the table, chairs scraping noisily on the concrete floors, and Dolly takes the bags and starts emptying the contents on the table. It would seem she went to quite a nice deli and perhaps also a bakery, and got baguettes and butter and several meats and cheese, in addition to the sparkling waters that Garnet is drinking. This is not how I pictured discussing our next job, I did think that it would simply be in my flat, but Dolly is right; that isn't typically how we do things. If there ever is a way we typically do things. We do think on our feet quite often.

There is something companionable about sharing a meal like this, it was sweet of Dolly to do so but also a surprisingly subtle gesture, smart of her to think of. She and Bits are looking at something on the table, perhaps speaking through their earpieces subvocally, as sometimes Bits squints and Dolly nods, but without locating the AR glasses in my purse, it's invisible to me. I glance at Will, who is watching them and thus can presumably see.

After a little while, when we are done picking at our picnic, Bits says "Okay, so I've got the plans for the casino. They seem pretty up to date, it wasn't built all that long ago and there've only been a few work permits since then, for things like adding a door or whatever, and they're all updated in the documentation. The main floor is where most of the sculptures are, mostly in the big open entryway, but there are some on the floor out where the slots are, and some on the next floor. I've watched the resets with the handcarts and people in jumpsuits, and the staff they use for that is bigger than our team but not much; if we're missing those couple of people, it won't be noticeable. There is active security, armed and trained, recertified every year. The managers don't really pay a lot of attention to the art installation stuff, they're paying attention to the employees in the cage, and the dealers, that kind of thing."

"The cigarette girls," Dolly says, opening a fizzing can of something and licking the foam off her thumb. "Or isn't that a French thing?"

"I think that's still just a Vegas thing," Bits says.

"Do we all speak French?" I ask suddenly. "Will that matter?"

"I can get by," Dolly says. It's Dolly whom I was asking about, really. We haven't spent much time together in French-speaking environments. "And artists and art installation people come from all over. Even America." She winks at me as she takes a drink from her can.

"So we will need jumpsuits, not dresses," Garnet says, uneasy in the face of Dolly's chaos. "And vans? How big are the sculptures."

"Big enough that some of them need two people to manage," Bits says. "There are some smaller, and a couple that are partly mechanical?"

"What, a robot diamond that walks onto its own transport?" Perry asks.

Bits shrugs. "Something like that. Maybe just their head moves?"

"So it is to our benefit that Will is participating," I say, putting a comforting hand on his arm. He does not do well idle, and in a city. We ought to have a place in the countryside, where he might putter about on property and have little projects with which to occupy himself. I could have a garden, with staff to maintain it of course, but planning it would be quite the diversion. The French countryside might not be the best for us, though, we might want someplace with milder winters. Or perhaps not, I've never before considered the French country winter.

"Yeah, it's good to have a big strong man around," Dolly says, grinning and elbowing Will, who laughs out of surprise or a self-preservative impulse to humor Dolly.

"My mother always said that's why she had boys, so that anytime she needed to rearrange the house, we'd be handy," he says, perhaps surprising even himself, and Dolly laughs.

"What a peach," she says. "Actually, speaking of cigarettes, anybody else want one?" She gets out a pack and offers it around, everybody declining but Perry. She knows better than to offer it to Bits or I and yet still does.

"Where will we get jumpsuits?" I ask.

"Well aren't you the fashionista, Bristles? Where will you get jumpsuits?"

"We can hardly have them made, that would be too glaring a clue in the event of our pursuit," I say, thinking again of that little fashion house storefront.

"Aw, I'm sure I can pop over to Germany and rustle something up," Dolly says. "Me and Perry can take a road trip, get used to each other's driving."

"Oh! We could do that." Perry is surprised, eager. Desperate for Dolly's approval and to prove themselves.

"Plus, there might be some, uh, armaments that we'll wanna have on hand." Dolly winks, turning away, and Perry exhales an absolute gust of smoke that cannot hide their blush from me.

"I'll trust you to take care of that, Dolly darling," I say. "Bits, what would our ideal, successful go at this look like, time-wise? We would enter the casino as a work crew at..."

"At eleven p.m. That's when they've been doing the reset. They go through and cover all of the statues, and then four pairs with hand carts shift them about, often removing some and adding others that were in storage. They finish their reset by one a.m. Nobody lingers, they don't take any breaks, they don't even really talk all that much, that I can tell, unless they're subvocal. They aren't in communication with casino security other than to say hi at the beginning of the night and to say they're leaving before they go out that back door, which then closes and the lock cycles."

"So, the six of us instead of eight, taking three hours to remove all of the statues. We can replace them with decoys, since security will not be expecting complete removal?"

"Are you askin' us or tellin' us?" Dolly asks, blowing a smoke ring.

"It was the idea that I had," I say smoothly. "Do we think that it's utterly ridiculous, or would it work?"

"It could work, I think," Garnet says. Perhaps she thinks that I need backup, sweet girl. She almost certainly feels the odd unbalance in the air between Dolly and myself. It troubles me, in a way nothing else has. "I was looking online at the statues, and some are really big? I don't know how we'd cover that the way they do."

Organically, in a somewhat comical manner, we all turn to Bits. She was the one, after all, who said no initially. She pauses, and we wait, and then she nods. "Well okay, I just found the plans for the carts that they used, and that mechanism is really easy, I could kitbash a few of those."

"Okay, so we get the vans. We get the jumpsuits. We get there at eleven, do our handshake with security, most of us shuffle the covered empty boxes with the covered diamond encrusted statues, get 'em back out to the vans, doors closed and on the road by one." Dolly ticks the things off on her hands, and some of us are nodding, Bits is frowning. "What about the people who are *supposed* to be handling the art?"

"Oh," Perry says.

"Oh is right," Dolly says, looking at Bits. "If they could be bought off, we wouldn't be having this meeting, right?"

"If they could be bought off, it'd be for more cost than the job is worth," Bits says.

"So what then? Car trouble? Tranquilizer darts? Shipping container?" Dolly's laughing-but-serious. "We gotta derail them for three hours, in such a way that they won't call anybody to let them know something's wrong. Because obviously we can't both be there."

"Do they do the reset every night?" Will asks. "Can we just add us into the schedule on an off night?"

"They do it every night," Bits says. "I can make it so they can't call anybody, but sustaining that for three hours, and running all our stuff at the casino is too much."

"What about like, Nautical Deborah? Somethin' like that an option?"

"We'd have to cut anybody else in and..."

"Nautical Deborah?" I raise my eyebrows and look from Bits and Dolly to Will, who shrugs.

"One o' Bitsy's hacker pals," Dolly says. "She's on an oil platform."

"Oh," I say faintly.

"Maybe I can call in a favor," Garnet says eventually. "Somebody who can keep the artist team occupied, unharmed, and then send them on their way after."

"Occupied how?" Dolly asks.

"Well if police were to pull them over, they could easily waste that much time searching vans and phones and things."

"You got police at your beck and call?" Dolly asks, hanging another cigarette on her lip.

"Not in general, no. But a single favor from somebody *like* police..."

"Bitsy, you vetted everybody, right?" Dolly asks, breaking off and turning.

"Dolly, that is very rude," I say.

"Uh-huh."

"I did, yeah," Bits says. "Garnet isn't an undercover agent."

"What are you then? Somebody's informant? The mayor's daughter? The lost dauphin's great great great niece? That' s not enough generations." She winks at me. "You know what I mean."

"I used to do street work," Garnet says evenly. "And I didn't want to keep doing street work. And so I informed on the worst person I knew." It seems only polite, fitting, to let some silence spin out in the room after that. From Perry's non-reaction, they already knew. From Dolly's raised eyebrows, she's thinking on the implications of Garnet's statement. Will keeps himself to himself, and after a moment, I clasp my hands together with a soft clap.

"Does that explanation suffice, Dolly?" I ask, smiling just so.

"Guess it does," she says, and lights her cigarette.

Chapter Six

With our rudimentary plan in place, we don't linger long after. It gets dark so dreadfully early this time of year, but what better place to spend it in than the City of Lights. Will and I make our way to the main thoroughfares again, walking together in companionable silence. He matches his stride to mine, and I feel him looking at me sometimes, for reassurance, perhaps, or to see that I don't require anything. I know that he is acclimating to this different kind of freedom that he has; I know that when we were in Morocco, Bits did what she calls deprogramming, and though Will had not seemed terribly programmed to me, he has a vulnerability now, like a man who no longer has the same calluses that he did for the tool that he must use. I feel certain that he will eventually talk about it, but I do not wish to pry. It's important for feelings like that to come in their own time, and the impulse may not be forced.

We've paused so that I can admire the mannequins on display in a resale shop window when I say, "Oh."

"Oh?" Will asks.

"Dolly and Perry don't have our measurements; how are they to buy jumpsuits for us?" I start to pull my phone out of my purse, but I pause when I see Will's bemused expression.

"I think they come in pretty broad sizes," he says, with a care that tells me he's keeping laughter out of his voice.

"Well I'm certain they do, depending on the type one buys. I've seen some exceedingly shapeless—"

"Bristol, that's part of the disguise." He hesitates, and then takes my hand, and we keep walking. "You were thinking about how much you love a costume," he says, allowing himself to smile this time. "You can't stand to blend in."

"That does make this sort of job difficult for me," I admit after a moment. "Perhaps it would be better if I was acting as a casino goer instead, in case a distraction is necessary." I can almost hear Dolly screeching at the notion that I'm immediately changing the plan.

"Maybe you can wear something like that under your jumpsuit and do a quick change if they—if we suddenly need a femme fatale." He is humoring me, of course, but it is an intriguing suggestion.

"What a splendid idea, darling, I'll think on that." We pause again, by a fountain. There are cafes lining the square, the doors flung open and the murmur of diners and the sounds of music and silverware echoing on the stone buildings and sidewalks. The glimmer of coins in the fountain catches my eye, like silver fishes darting there in all the lights, and I pause to look a moment before dipping into my purse. It isn't *uncommon* for me to have cash money, but it isn't common either. In America, I almost never do; in Europe, I more often do, and I find, paradoxically, an old American quarter, the eagle on it worn nearly smooth.

Will watches me, wondering but not questioning, and I hold the quarter for a moment, thinking on my wish. It isn't enough, I think, to wish for a successful job; I haven't many worries about that, actually. Especially not with Dolly back with us. No, what I wish for is the unspoken, invisible rift in our little trio to be fixed, or to heal itself over, so that we might continue again more comfortably. I think of the look on Butler's face when he opened the door and saw me, and squeeze the quarter a moment, then give it a little toss into the water, where it makes its soft splash and becomes one of the darting fishes for a moment.

"I don't know if I've ever wished in a fountain," Will says.

"Not even when you were small?" I ask, turning to him, wide-eyed. "Oh darling, you must." I hunt for another coin, this time a silver dirham from Morocco, and I press it into his palm. "Now don't tell me what it is, just picture it in your mind, and when you're ready, throw it into the fountain."

"Alright," he says, agreeable, amused. I like this Will better than the watchful Will who isn't quite sure of his place in the world. His confidence was shaken so thoroughly both when we absconded with him and then after the unpleasantness in Morocco. That I have not been fully privy to, and thought we were simply all putting behind us. Until Dolly stayed away for so long. I'm not used to dwelling on the past; I'm used to putting it firmly behind me as I walk towards my carefully crafted vision of the future.

It is not the best time to ask, now and without preparation, but also it is a very nice time to ask because Will will not be expecting me to, and his unguarded first reaction will speak volumes. Still I wait, though, watching him bounce the coin in his hand a bit as he thinks, his eyes on the fountain, or on the cafe just beyond, his thoughts I cannot begin to guess where.

Then he does close his hand around the coin for a moment, as though wrapping his wish about it, and gives it a toss into the fountain. We stand a moment longer before he offers his arm, which I accept, and we continue walking in companionable silence. "Will, what happened in Morocco?" I ask when we are almost to our flat, tipping my face up to his.

His eyebrows go up in surprise, briefly, and his mouth gives a sudden and unhappy twist, before he blinks a few times in rapid succession and commands his features again. "I want you to understand that my hesitation isn't because I don't want to tell you, but because I don't know what to tell."

"That's very interesting," I say.

"The whole story isn't mine to tell," he says, when I don't continue or expand upon my question. "So you'll need to talk to Dolly and Bits about that. But..." We stop at our door, and he taps in the code before holding it open for me to go up ahead of him. Bits strenuously objected to my using an electronic lock, but so long as I agreed to her surveilling my entrance to make sure that it is I or Will or a legitimate entry, she acquiesced. I do prefer keys, of course, but I just had to have this flat, it's absolutely perfect. The door closes behind us, shutting out the street, the lights, and I ascend the stairs lightly, aware of him just behind me. I open the inner door with a key, an affectation I quite enjoy, and allow him to take my coat and purse. "Do you want a drink? I do."

"If you'd like." I follow him into the sitting room and arrange myself on one of the chairs there, wingbacked and a deep chocolate colored velvet with fanciful patterns embroidered into it in similarly-colored thread. I watch him pour himself a whiskey, and then do a gin and tonic for me. Not the proper mood for a champagne cocktail. He brings me my glass, remains standing as he sips his whiskey, not looking at me but not looking out the window either. Once he pours his second whiskey is when he starts.

"Morocco was a bad time," he says slowly. I think perhaps he's been considering this moment, when he might be asked to explain himself, or his part in the goings on. "The Agency doesn't just let people go like this, you know. People retire, or switch agencies, and sometimes, rarely, people are injured or killed, but this kind of leaving has never happened. So obviously they were going to come for me. Especially since they didn't know yet if I did anything while I still had my clearances."

He pauses, and I sip my drink. It is a lovely gin, not something I'm always given to drinking, but when I am in the proper mood, I am quite fond of it. "We didn't exactly give you the luxury of saying goodbye, darling, that is true."

He gives a short laugh, a little bitter. "No, my choices were much more limited than that." He tosses back the rest of the whiskey in a short, ugly gesture. He sets the glass down, removes his fingers from it precisely. He is, I think, thinking that he would like a third and that he will not have a third. He turns to me. "Getting you to safety was the primary thought, especially after what happened...before. With Homeland." He watches my face, on which I maintain a schooled blankness. I am not predisposed to talking about what happened with Homeland. "After that, the guess was that I would be debriefed and then, uh, decommissioned, which was a correct guess. One of the local hotels had sublevels that the agency used, that Bits got intel on."

"So they debriefed you," I prompt. "But when you say de-commissioned, you are not, I think, speaking of this sort of ex-pat retirement?"

"No, I'm using the sanitized term for being executed as a risk too great to allow free." He looks into my eyes steadily as he says this, unhappy at this reality.

"And yet here you stand."

"Because the rest of our plan, mostly Bits I guess, was very simple. Dolly came to extract me."

We look at each other for several moments, those possibilities unspooling in my mind. Butler saying *If you let her get hurt like that again*. What had she done, for Will's sake and thus for mine? What had been done *to* her? "I see," I say carefully.

Will's expression softens; he does not want to be cruel to me. To hurt me. "Dolly is very good at what she does," he says. "And she had Bits reactivate her for it."

"*Oh*," I say, not intending to, the syllable tearing free from my lips of its own accord. Dolly, once deactivated, depro-grammed, with the material we got from that final old black site, said she never wanted that to happen to her again. Never wanted to be *separate* from those feelings. "Oh." I say again.

"So it's not a surprise that she didn't tell you, I guess. Maybe it's a surprise that you didn't, uh, correspond, but she was giving you your space, from what Bits said."

"Giving me my space," I repeat slowly. I did say I would never forgive her. Is that why she would do something like that, reactivate her super soldier programming, with the risks that it might entail, for *me*? It's disingenuous to ask myself that question. Yes, it is why. Dolly's loyalty to me, and to Bits, for all our bickering, has been unshakable. "I never thought she would...This does clarify some things for me, I suppose." Butler's face. Her frustrated, amused anger at saying thank you to her. My unwillingness to be free with my emotions in an unguarded way. "Oh, darling, I'm so sorry you went through that."

"Me? I had a cakewalk compared to Dolly," he says. "I mean, I did think that Clancy was going to drive me out into the desert and put one behind my ear, or that Harding was going to shoot me and then drop me into some hole that they'd then fill with concrete, but those were known risks when I chose to come with you instead of dying in that hotel room in Las Vegas."

"I am sorry about that," I say, truly contrite. "But you *must* understand, darling, that enough was enough and—"

"No, now, don't go apologizing for that either," he says, setting my drink aside and taking my hands in his. "Since I didn't see you yell at Dolly and slap her, so I can say this is the most upset I've ever seen you."

"I'm perfectly composed," I say stiffly.

"You are, but also by this point I know you at least a little." He smiles ruefully. "Maybe you want to try talking to Dolly?"

"Not tonight," I say automatically, but he doesn't press me on that.

"No, not tonight. Maybe not even before the job. But clearing the air will do you both some good, I think." His hands are warm, and comforting.

"Yes, it very much would," I say, and my tone is final enough that he moves aside to let me stand, as though we're closing the conversation like a book. "Thank you for indulging me, darling," I say. "It was more than a little gauche of me to ambush you in this manner."

"Less gauche than asking what I wished for," he says, his smile easier this time. But he does go and pour a third whiskey.

Chapter Seven

Coming from America, it is still very amusing to me that one could say "we'll just pop over to Germany for this errand" as though going to the seaside for the day. But that is what Dolly and Perry do the next day.

//I'm keeping tabs,// Bits messages me, unprompted.

//I have every faith that they will be fine,// I say as I am finishing my makeup. I am going to a fashion showing, just a very small party in Marquis' gallery. The catering is with a small, competent operation they've contracted before, petit-fours and other little delights simply to *die* for. I've just misted on my perfume when Will appears in my doorway.

"Your car is here," he says. Our eyes meet in the mirror, briefly, and I smile.

"Thank you, darling. You know you're invited to this as well?"

"I know," he says stiffly.

I pause a moment, and then say, "It would be very rude to Marquis if you continue to decline their invitations."

Will hesitates in the door, not frozen exactly but calculations clear on his face. "Give me ten," he says finally.

"It would be perfectly sweet of you." I don't know how this situation with Will will end up in the long run, but I am enjoying the dalliance. Or, approaching a dalliance; I've kissed him on the cheek, and he's put his arm around me, and offers me his arm when we walk, but it's all been very chaste. Poor lamb, what would he have done if we went through all this and then I left him to his own devices?

In ten minutes, we meet at the front door. He's shaved, and put on a nicer shirt, but not a tie. I wonder how many of his ten minutes were taken up by this deliberation; it was the correct choice.

I skim my messages on the ride to Marquis'. Advertisements of sales, an invitation to another gallery opening, an invitation to a girl's night next month at a club that I've frequented only occasionally. They would like for me to be a more regular member, and while I am not against it, I also am not entirely convinced of its benefit to me. Nicolai with a chatty message which is something of a surprise, and Suzette with an even longer message that also, casually, asks at the end if I've heard from Nicolai lately. This brings Nicolai's missive into different focus, and I'll ask Dolly if his love life is something she's ever been aware of.

I can always rely on Marquis to give me a lovely welcome, and they have a cocktail and a corsage for me the second I'm in the door. "Alone?" they ask, once we've kissed.

"Will is checking our coats," I say.

"He *was* invited too," Marquis says in surprised delight.

"I *did* remind him of that, darling! You know how he's been, so I was pleased he decided to come along after all."

"I do indeed. Maybe he'll relax one day...I'm sure we could help him with that." Marquis winks, and I keep careful rein on my expression.

"While I'm certain we could, it is much more interesting to see what he decides on his own." I sip my drink; I do know that I can trust Marquis, in this regard. Actually, this is the first time I've heard them make such a distasteful joke.

"I suppose that's true," they say, not noticing any change in my demeanor, which was my intent. "I've been thinking you've been hiding him away all to yourself, but really, he's been sheltering while adjusting, hasn't he?"

"Just so."

"And you?" Marquis arches a brow at me, and I return the gesture.

"And me?"

"How are *you* adjusting? You haven't had a steady in—"

I wave a hand. "Oh, we aren't anything like that." They laugh. "No, really. I could hardly take advantage of his state, it wouldn't be fair at *all*."

"Like a lamb to the slaughter, I thought that was the appeal." Marquis plucks a drink for themself off a passing tray. "And here he is."

Will crosses the room to us, eyes on me but also checking corners and vectors and whatever nonsense he and Dolly concern themselves with. "Marquis, thanks for the invitation."

"Will, such a pleasure to see you again! Our chairs are here."

It's too small a space for there to actually be a proper VIP area separate from the rest of the seating and staging, but these chairs are a bit separate, and have better cushioning. There isn't exactly a runway, of course, but the gallery is longer than it is wide, and Marquis is able to make do very well. The designer also sits with us, a fluttery French woman named Amandine, and her theme was transformation, she explained in her little introduction before the models start walking. Everything is very flowy and ethereal, with convertible elements. One of the girls is in a short skirt that, when she twirls, lengthens into a train. One of the gentlemen has what at first seems like a plain jumpsuit, and the top of it turns to a very structured vest while the bottom unzips into a skirt, and I can't exactly see the trick of where the *sleeves* go, and I turn to Amandine in delight.

"You're so very clever!" I exclaim, sotto voce.

She's frowning critically as she watches the models, but gives me a distracted smile. "Oh, thank you my dear, you are too kind. I'm not certain some of these pieces were exactly ready, but I had to fill everything out."

"No, the jumpsuit, it's *everything*." I think of Dolly and Perry, on the road to Germany. Or perhaps on the road back now, who's to say. I put that into their capable hands. Will shifts just slightly in his seat behind me, but I don't think he shall interrupt.

"Do you really think so?" From her tone, she's used to effusive, disingenuous flattery.

"I *do*, yes! I would be wild to have one, are they in production at all?" It's wicked of me to ask; I *did* agree to the plan. This is simply a contingency consideration, surely I couldn't be faulted for that.

"*You* would like one?" She looks at me more fully, then, and leans past me to address Marquis. "Is she serious, your friend? She would want one of my pieces?"

"Bristol wants what Bristol wants," Marquis says, convincing, curious. Our eyes meet briefly and I smile. "She's got the money, if that's what you mean."

"Tsk, as if I would be so crass. We are having a civilized conversation, Marquis." She leans back in her chair again and smiles at me. "Would you like to be fitted? I have a prototype that is near to your size, that could be finished without much trouble."

"I wouldn't *dream* of letting you go to the trouble without paying for—"

"We can come to an understanding," she says. Her eyes are sharp and bright, and I return her smile.

"Then yes, I would love to be fitted, thank you for the opportunity."

"Here, my card. Tomorrow?"

"Tomorrow would be lovely." I tuck her card into my purse, and we watch the rest of the show, before the space is reset for mingling and hors d'oeuvres.

At one point, Marquis grasps my arm and says, "Don't look now, but the *most* devastatingly handsome man just walked in."

"If I'm not supposed to *look*, darling..." I say, smiling indulgently. I do think that Will is looking, but in such a subtle way that Marquis doesn't catch it.

"I'll describe him to you, and then you can look." They wait for my nod, glancing over my shoulder again, and say, "He's extremely tall, and his hair is just inky black, like the middle of the night. He's got a bit of a five o'clock shadow, you can practically hear his beard growing, it must be quite the chore for him. He's dressed either carelessly or expensively, I can't tell from here. Chiseled cheekbones, bright eyes."

"You paint a delightful picture," I say, thinking that he *almost* sounds like Butler, who would not have followed Dolly to Paris if he hadn't come in the first place. "May I look now?"

"Yes, tell me how I did." Marquis finishes their drink, and I turn to look. Not Butler, and I'm strangely relieved. Will would have reacted if it was Butler. No matter, it isn't anything I would ever need to tell Dolly, or indeed everybody. Quite handsome, just as Marquis described. There's something about his bearing, though...

"Oh, darling, I do think he's a police officer. Or perhaps governmental agent, INTERPOL or some such." Not Will's agency, not dressed like that. I didn't see a single one of those men know a thing about fabrics other than synthetics, presumably because that way they don't have to know how to iron. I place my hand on Will's sleeve, and when I feel how tense he is, I tip my head slightly to look up at him. He looks down at me and smiles tightly. Nothing *new* wrong, I don't think.

"What a shame. Unless this is my opportunity to get my own secret agent man." They bump shoulders with me and we both laugh, which comes at a lull in the room's conversation and makes the tall, handsome man look in our direction.

"Now's your opportunity," I say softly. "And I think I'll take my leave. I do have my fitting in the morning. Will, darling, get our coats?" He nods and moves off, pointedly not looking at tall, dark, and handsome.

Marquis makes a face. "In the *morning*? Not such a privilege after all."

"And yet we endure." I kiss their cheek and wave farewell to Amandine and take one final look at the model in the transformed jumpsuit before we slip out.

We must wait a moment in the street for the car service to come around, and I check my lipstick in a compact and watch

Will watching me. When I put it away, he says, "It's probably good that you made me go."

"I didn't make you," I say with a little laugh.

"You strongly suggested," he says, smiling unhappily. "But isolating myself isn't good. So thank you."

"You're welcome," I say.

It's quite late when we get back, but I'm also certain that Bits is sometimes in VR instead of sleeping, and I message her //Did Dolly and Perry have a nice trip?//

I've removed my jewelry and placed it in its boxes before she answers. //Yeah, they got us all jumpsuits and some other stuff to make us look convincing. I'm watching the installation crew on the cameras right now, and sometimes they have measuring tapes and hammers and things, though I haven't seen any of them use them.//

//They are part of the installation, as we said.//

//I guess.//

//Will we meet, to make sure the jumpsuits fit?//

//We can't meet too often, you know, it'll draw attention.//

I roll my eyes, if only because she cannot see me doing it. Rarely do I indulge in the childish gesture. //Yes I know, darling, it's why we stopped meeting at my flat and why we instead go to your warehouse hideaway. But also the jumpsuits aren't of any use to us if they don't fit.//

Another pause, probably conferring with the others. I realize that we haven't touched our group chat since before Morocco. //Tomorrow evening? After dark.//

//Thank you for humoring me.// She sends back an emoji meant to be an assent I'm sure, and I simply leave that read. It's when Bits is spending more time conversing with her hacker acquaintances that her text diction slips in that direction, and it isn't within my lexicon, nor do I care for it to be.

After dark should be plenty of time for my fitting to be sorted, and to retrieve Will. Perhaps I should arrange for a meal, it would only be fair. I imagine arriving with a tremendous load of hamburgers, to satisfy Bits and Dolly's tastes, and laugh softly. The need for secrecy precludes having an actual caterer the way I'd like, of course.

I consider messaging Dolly but am struck with uncharacteristic hesitation. What would I say? We don't normally message each other anyway. I think about Will's reticence to talk about Morocco, on her behalf. I think of Butler's face.

I change into a pajama set and then remove my makeup and wash my face before applying my serums, which smell lightly of green tea. I cannot abide too strong a scent on my face when I am going to sleep, and it would cling to my pillowcases and build up and be unbearable. I take my hair down from its updo, setting the pins aside and brushing it out with my wooden handled, boar bristle brushes. I don't tend to do one hundred strokes per night, but it isn't unheard of. It's very good for the hair, and also soothing. Nothing has happened, I don't need to be soothed. I pick up my phone again, no message from Dolly. A long message from Marquis, detailing their interaction with the stranger, who is apparently spending the night. A notification of a trunk sale next week.

I can hear Will moving about in the flat; I think he's probably gotten changed as well, and he has been in the habit of having a nightcap. I don't know if that's a new habit, or one that he picked up since his closer association with us. I could ask Bits, she would have some way of knowing. Liquor store receipts, or bar surveillance. I do enjoy wondering upon these things on my own, though; facts needn't always enter the mix.

On impulse, I pull on a little wrapper and leave my room, catching Will by surprise as he turns from the liquor cabinet, drink in hand. "Was I too loud?" he asks. "I didn't mean to bother you."

"You aren't a bother, darling," I say, dropping into one of the chairs and tucking my feet up. "Will you mix me something nice?"

"Something nice," he repeats, smiling. "I can hardly refuse." He sets down his drink and considers the bottles, and then our glasses, before selecting a martini glass, and mixes me a drink.

"Thank you, darling," I say, when he's handed me the glass.

"You're welcome." He stands nearby for a moment, then gets his drink and sits in the chair nearest mine. "I assume we've got plans tomorrow?"

"I have my fitting with the designer in the morning, and I won't torment you by making you go, and then we will be meeting Bits and Dolly after dark to check the jumpsuits and I think repeat the plan, to make sure we all know our roles."

"Bits did send me information about the casino, so I'd know the layout," he says. "Since Perry and Dolly will be driving, I guess it's good to have me to move things."

"Just so." I sip my drink, which is very...*refreshing* shall we say, as he's made me a lemon drop. Perhaps he meant to do a Champs-Élysées. It is a *good* lemon drop, simply not what I was expecting, but the lighting is not such in this room at the moment that he senses anything amiss.

We sit in what I think is companionable silence for a time, but then he does start to fidget, especially once he's run out of his drink. He wants to pour another one for the sake of something to do with himself, I think, but also he doesn't want to drink much more. We did imbibe somewhat at the gallery, after all. And Will is doing what he can to regain a sense of control over his life, or at least his choices.

He waits until I've finished my drink, though, before rising to take both our glasses. There's a little dishwasher in the kitchen for when we *do* eat or drink things here, and I think that most of the time, what it handles is our alcohol accoutrement. "I'll be right back," he says, lingering.

"I'll be waiting," I say. I do like this room in the flat quite a lot, I think I was very successful with the decorations, in making it feel plush and comfortable. Will's bedroom, I did the broad strokes on but have left him to his own devices otherwise, and of course my bedroom is my favorite. I've even considered having my Fabergé egg brought here from Morocco, but haven't yet. Despite everything that happened at my hotel, those were extreme circumstances; it is otherwise very secure, and such things are unlikely to happen a second time. Besides the fact that my *belongings* were never the targets in question.

I listen to him go down the hall, listen to the distant clink of the glasses in the rack. The water runs a moment, perhaps he's having a glass of that as well, and then another glass. He's still dressed for going out, but I suppose that's the nature of men and their clothes. Will is not exactly the sweat pants or lounge suit kind of man, and I might be a teensy bit horrified if he was. He returns, and smiles again when he sees me still sitting there, as I'd said.

"I'm going to come right out and admit it," he says. "I don't know where to take things from here."

"Your secret is of course safe with me," I say, and hold my hand out to him. He comes and takes it, a little bemused, and I rise to my feet.

"I appreciate it," he says. He didn't step back when I stood, so his confidence really is returning, and he also hasn't yet released my hand. "Bristol, I—"

On impulse, I step closer and kiss him full on, much in the way I did the first time we said goodbye, in that old bus station. He's extremely surprised, but does not break the kiss, putting his other arm around me. Perhaps he's thought about this moment, when it would come. If it would come.

When we do finally part, breathless, we stay much like that, very little space between us, looking into each other's eyes. "Perhaps that was wicked of me," I murmur, giving him the opportunity to excuse himself.

"No," he says. "No, I...I've been hoping for it."

"I don't kiss just anybody."

"I know," he says, and kisses me again.

Chapter Eight

I slip out of the flat next morning fairly early, leaving Will in what seems to be a very restful sleep. Perhaps his most restful since we took him away from everything he knew. I take a moment to leave him a note, lightly scented, bidding him good morning. He's aware of my morning plans and is unlikely to think I'll have abandoned him, but it seems the correct touch. Of course, he can always message me. Or message Bits, to have her locate me. Bits is obviously more than a glorified switchboard operator, but also often performs that function with such apparent ease that it's equally easy to rely upon her for it. But also I want to spare him the sudden fear of abandonment and the dread that the messages may not go through.

I have my morning coffee at a cafe that I fancy before going to Amandine's storefront; she is also a seamstress of a more mundane, everyday sort, and while there are people of her ilk who repair clothing, if you know how to find them, I'm certain that few of them are of her caliber. She has a drowsy looking shopgirl who starts to come and greet me once I'm through the door, but she swiftly interposes, taking both my hands in hers and looking me up and down. "Yes, I'm certain I have one nearly your measurements already, you may be able to go home with it today if you are willing to laze about with me for a short time." She's speaking in rapid French, but French is my most fluent language after English, especially with how much time I've spent here.

"You are my only appointment this morning," I say, charmed.

"Hannah, put the tea on," she says, and leads me to the back of the shop with a gesture.

I've had ever so many fittings in recent years, some before we stole the diamonds that really made our fortunes, and most after. Amandine is such a light touch with her measuring tape, she's a dream to work with. I've also been to fittings where no physical measurements were taken, and it was all electronic, but I confess, I do prefer many old fashioned things. We get too far away from ourselves otherwise, I think.

I wait, still standing on the stool, as she goes away to the racks, runs her hand along the hangers, and comes up with the jumpsuit she had in mind. "There, take this, the dressing room is behind you."

"Merci, madame."

The dressing room seems it was once a closet, now repurposed. The mirror is kind, and the lighting excellent; I take an indulgent moment to preen before changing. Once I am changed, I'm not certain what adjustments I would require, though also I'm unsure of the transformative mechanism of the piece, other than the zips in the legs.

"It is nearly correct," she says, furrowing her brow and pursing her lips as she looks at me. "I need to adjust it here and here," she touches the places. "But let me show you." We stand in front of her triptych of mirrors and that is when I become aware of the cunningly hidden seams and fastenings, the way the fabric folds in on itself and becomes the other garment. I'll need different underpinnings for this, but it is so fun, so clever.

"I'm so delighted, thank you so much," I say, as I change back into my clothes and hand over the jumpsuit for its alterations.

//You're up early,// Bits says in my ear, distracting me from Amandine's reply as she whisks herself away.

//I had an impulse meeting with a fashion designer.// I accept a cup of tea from the assistant and settle into one of the plush chairs that the waiting area has to offer. There are a number of couture magazines here, and I select one to thumb through. //Will and I went to her show at Marquis' gallery last night, and I just *had* to have one of her pieces.//

//Oh, Will went? Good for him.//

//I suggested Marquis' feelings might be hurt should Will keep declining their invitations.//

//I see.// I cannot tell if Bits is amused by this, or disapproves and thinks I ought to have left Will to his own devices. He is making an effort, after all. It's possible that, after myself, she's spent the most time with him. No, not just possible, but simply true. She met with him daily to deprogram him in Morocco. The deep state programming, anyway; we all of us have our social programming that is far more difficult to overcome, especially in so short a time.

//Perhaps it was wicked of me, but it *did* seem to do him some good.//

//If you say so.// The message equivalent of a shrug, trés Bits.

//Is there anything you'd like me to bring tonight?// It's possible that the girls would disapprove of my trying to bring dinner, thinking that I might draw too much attention in a way that Dolly would not. I'm also anticipating Bits looking into my designer as we speak.

//No, just you and Will. Thank you for asking.//

//You're welcome, darling.//

//Did you tell Marquis that they would be hearing from me?//

//I didn't have the chance, darling, but I'm sure they won't mind. It won't be a moment, to give you that contact information.//

//Just checking.//

When Amandine returns and I change again, she pronounces the jumpsuit perfect. In the mirror, untransformed, it looks remarkably like the ones I presume Dolly and Perry bought yesterday, to match the art crew's getups. A few snaps and folds, and the top is slightly different from those last night, but a structured, corset-like garment, and the pants flow with the other fabric to all appear rather dress-like.

"I love it," I say, clasping my hands and turning to her. "Won't you let me pay you?"

She waves a dismissive hand, but she is smiling. "It was a prototype and the show is done. What use is it, laying about? This way you can spread my name when people swarm to you and ask who you're wearing."

"You're so very generous, thank you! Of course I'll spread your name far and wide, and I hope to hear when you have new designs."

"I'll have Hannah put you in my book," she says, pleased. "Now get changed, and I will package this for you properly."

She shows me how to return the garment to its jumpsuit state, and leaves me to the dressing room again.

Shopping bag in my arm, I walk up the street and am considering whether I'd like a coffee when Garnet messages me. //Bristol, would you mind meeting to talk?//

//Of course we can meet, darling. Are you available now?// I look at the time; it has grown late enough that it would be a surprise if Will was still abed. Perhaps he is, or perhaps he's simply leaving me space to go about my errands and return.

//Yes. Would you like to try the cafe by the gardens? We spoke about it once before.//

//That would be lovely, darling, I'll make my way there.// I can only imagine that she wants to talk about Dolly. Our little Paris group hasn't had time at all to separately discuss Dolly's sudden presence in our lives, though of course to Bits and myself it's a return to status quo. I hadn't considered that, and perhaps I ought to have. But no, it's important to be able to think and adapt on your feet.

I *have* been the cafe by the gardens, and though not much is blooming just now, it's still a lovely, well-crafted space. Inside, Garnet has already claimed a table for us, and when I go to greet her, another cup of coffee is brought for me.

"I ordered your usual, I hope you don't mind?" Garnet says. My usual, lately, has been a simple dark roast café au lait.

"No, of course I don't mind, darling, that's very thoughtful of you." I set my handbag and shopping bag down in the empty seat, sit across from her. "Now, tell me what's bothering you."

"Well for starters, now I'm bothered that it was so obvious," she says with a little laugh that I know is her adaptation of my own. She hasn't done that very much, just a few subtle touches. Garnet is very much her own girl, and she's dreadfully clever when it comes to adding to her arsenal. She doesn't want to *be* me, she wants to be as effective as me on her own merit.

"It's very tricky indeed to slip anything past me." I sip my coffee, allowing her to take her time. The cafe is not terribly crowded; a few people drinking their morning mugs and perusing local papers.

"I wish I'd talked to you earlier, and less publicly, about how I'd done street work. Before I just threw it in Dolly's face like that. I feel like I didn't handle that in the best way."

I reach over and place my hand on her wrist a moment in comfort. "Oh darling, Dolly didn't think twice about what you said or how you said it, that just isn't how she is! You poor dear, were you really so worried?" Her silence speaks volumes. "Listen to me carefully: it doesn't matter what you once were. What matters is what you make of yourself."

"I'm just used to—"

"Barbaric responses, I'm absolutely certain! You needn't worry about that with Dolly, or Bits. Or me," I add hastily. "We none of us started this way."

"Thank you, Bristol," she says, and her smile is more collected now, less strained. "We didn't exactly fully go over each other's backgrounds when we got together "

"Nor would it have been appropriate. We knew what we needed to know, and now we know more. C'est la vie!" I sip my coffee. I do think that Bits already knew this about Garnet; she did do some amount of checking around on Garnet and Perry when we met and started doing little jobs together, if for no other reason than to make absolutely certain that a different shadow agency hadn't latched on to us. I also think Perry already knew, if only based on the length of their association.

"Well now I feel silly for making you come out," she says, starting to blush.

"Nonsense, it's important to act on such impulses. Would you have rathered it left to bother you, through the job? Of course not!" I smile and she mirrors it. "There, that's better. I'm glad you spoke to me immediately."

"I'm glad that it...doesn't matter. People change, when they find that out about me."

"If they change, then they are people you would not benefit from having around you anyway," I say firmly. "After all this, did you speak to your associate? Is he willing to play a part?"

"He is, and I looped Bits in. I guess we're meeting tonight? So we'll update then."

"I wanted to make absolutely certain that the jumpsuits fit," I say.

"That makes sense."

As we're finishing our coffee, chatting about less consequential things, I do get a text from Will. //Not to rush you, but I'm ordering lunch. I'll just get your usual?//

//That would be lovely darling, thank you.// I set my coffee cup down and dab my lips. "Well, I must be off. But we should do this more often."

"It was nice," Garnet says, smiling.

Chapter Nine

Lunch, and new flavors of the sparkling water that I favor, are waiting for me back at the flat. Will as well, mais oui, though I can tell that he is trying desperately not to seem expectant, or needy, or any different from usual.

We eat in companionable silence, ignoring the occasional gentle chimes of my phone, the noise that indicates the usual sorts of media alerts, not a message from anybody consequential. This is also the time of day Suzette might message me quite a lot, and while I value the maintained connection, it isn't necessary to reply to her immediately. She expects me to savor any gossip she's found for me.

As we're finishing, Will says, "Thank you for leaving me a note. I think I would've been in a bad spot otherwise."

"Of course, darling," I say, smiling. "I didn't want you to think I'd simply fled, after last night."

A pause, a long and interesting pause, and I do wonder what he's thinking. It isn't until he's clearing our dishes that he asks, "Are we going to talk about last night?"

I pause as well, but more briefly. "I'm not certain that we need to." My phone chimes again, but this time it is Bits. "I must take this, darling, I do apologize."

"It's okay. I'll be ready to go when you are," he says, and disappears to the kitchen.

As I answer the call, I take my shopping bag into my room, so that I can hang my jumpsuit up. "Yes, Bits darling?" Will made the bed when he got up, I note, and quite neatly. Oh goodness, what if that is what Bits is *calling* about, rather than messaging me. But how would she know? I nearly laugh.

"When you saw Garnet, did she say if she'd straightened out her end with that contact?"

"No, we didn't talk about that at all. Why?"

"Just checking."

"You never *call* me to just check." Of course I have a hanger for the jumpsuit, but it's a matter now of finding a place tall enough to hang out. I stand in place and turn around, assessing. "And why wouldn't you call her to ask?"

"Dolly told me to."

"That doesn't assuage my concerns, Bits darling." There is a sconce bolted to the wall that will be perfect. "What is Dolly's concern?"

"That Garnet's contact is maintaining contact in order to net other street criminals."

"Well, that's perfectly fine, we aren't *street* criminals," I say, laughing. Bits doesn't laugh with me, of course. "I assumed you'd already looked into all that."

"I mean, I did, but I can read people's tech, not their minds."

"None of us can read minds, and I'm not certain that would improve matters in most situations." For me, at least, it would ruin the game. Being able to untangle the social knots is a significant part of the fun. "While I appreciate your caution, we perhaps don't need to expect a double cross in this instance."

"I'm not going to just not worry about it?" Bits says.

"Nor would I ask you to! But I am not! If he's already agreed to delay or detain the *real* jumpsuit-wearing art installation people, and does so, that's all we need."

"Yes, it's the 'and does so' that we're so concerned with." I can hear Dolly in the background, but not what she's saying.

"I understand what you're concerned with, truly," I say. "But I'm not certain what you propose. We intend to perform the job tomorrow night, and Garnet's contact will already know that, if she followed the plan. Did she speak with him? Surely you know that much."

"She did, we just—"

"We just wanna make sure that you know you might be burning Paris for yourself," Dolly says, suddenly loud and clear. I can only imagine how close she is to Bits's microphone, or perhaps Bits brought her in on the call, that isn't my concern.

"Well of course that's been in my considerations, darling, I simply don't think it will happen." I think that the designer's jumpsuit might be wool, very finely woven, because there is not a wrinkle to be seen despite its time in the shopping bag. It also has a certain feel to it, and I run my hand down a sleeve again, thoughtfully. I perhaps have not given wool's versatility quite enough thought. "Why did you wait to bring this up, Dolly darling?"

"Well I didn't want to immediately crash your little disciple, first thing after getting here," she says.

"That's very kind of you. Did Perry say something yesterday, to raise this concern?"

A pause, maybe because of my particular segue, and then Dolly says, "I might've asked."

"Oh, Dolly."

"Not about *Garnet*, about her pet cop. Don't turn this around on me."

"And what did Perry *say*?"

"That this guy's the real deal and would cut off his arm for Garnet. It's like she's got her own Will."

"Oh don't say things like that, darling," I say, frowning even though this is only an audio call, and Dolly laughs.

"I'm not offended, they don't know about my arm."

"If you are confident in Perry's assessment, then I'm uncertain why we're having the conversation."

"Maybe I just wanted to make sure you weren't bored already."

"Then why have Bits call me under artifice? Honestly, Dolly, this isn't like you." Now is obviously not the time to ask her about Morocco. Not in a call.

A pause, probably her dragging on an ecigarette. "Maybe not."

"I think we just need a better built in QA period with our planning," Bits says. "I've been keeping tabs on Garnet's cop since we knew about him, and he seems straightforward enough that it's either genuine or a complete construct, and the effort that would take to lay a trap for just somebody to come by seems to rule that out."

"Then what is there to worry about? We can discuss it tonight, when we look at our costumes. Dolly, you and Perry also have our vehicle considerations handled?"

A pause; perhaps Dolly is constructing a reason that Garnet is actually an operative from another agency, who was the perfect bait for me when I needed others in the game. Perhaps Perry is involved; Perry is like Garnet's Dolly, if that policeman is her Will. If we are pursuing this metaphor, which is actually making me a bit uneasy, to my surprise.

"Maybe I just thought you'd pay attention to Bitsy's logic instead o' my gut."

"Is your...gut...genuinely telling you that Garnet or her policeman are not to be trusted?"

"Not exactly, but I'm not sure what I'm hung up on. Other'n whatever little extra thing you got planned."

I laugh, surprised, delighted. "Dolly darling, whatever do you mean." More of her 'gut,' or just Bits knowing where we all are at all times.

She laughs too, short, rueful. "Right."

"So about tonight," Bits says, the only one on the line again.

"What about tonight?"

"We thought we've already had too much back and forth here, and so we'll just meet earlier tomorrow to get ready."

"Did something happen?" They should have *said*, if that was the case. Dolly's gut indeed.

"No, we just came to our senses."

"But—" It surprises me, how disappointed I am to not see them tonight after all.

"It's just good OpSec, Bristol, please." There's unspoken words there. 'For once,' perhaps, given prior comments on my behavior leading up to a job.

"I'll agree, provided you promise that I won't meet you tomorrow and discover that you've already done the job," I say smoothly. My own pre-job behavior aside, they *did* do that to me once, the scoundrels.

"I promise," Bits says solemnly, very slightly different from her normal tone. "We need everybody for this."

"I suppose we'll just use a whole mess of safety pins, if necessary," I say.

"We've got those," Bits says, obviously relieved.

"I shall see you tomorrow, then, at the rendez-vous."

"And no extra funny business!" Dolly yells in the background. "From any of us!"

"Fingers crossed," I say, laughing, though I do feel slightly bereft when I hang up. Canceled plans are rarely to be celebrated.

I sit at my dressing-table and consider my hair. A French twist should do; it's been a very good, no fuss style to keep my hair out of the way during a job. Makeup, my usual smudge-proof, waterproof, lightly made up option will do. Jewelry...I'm certain I have a necklace that will both be hidden by the done-up jumpsuit and also be decoration enough so as not to need earrings, so that if I must transform my jumpsuit into evening-wear, the lack of certain pieces won't seem too unusual.

Will knocks at my door. "Bits messaged me that we're all just staying in tonight," he says.

"Yes, I just spoke with them." I turn in my seat. "If you'd like, you can open the door."

"Thanks." He does, but lingers in the doorway. He's holding something just out of sight. "I thought you might like to make up for tonight, so I ordered dinner from the bistro with the chicken you like."

I tilt my head slightly. "That bistro doesn't deliver, darling."

"I know," Will says, his smile a return to the confident one he had at our first meeting. He shifts his position, holds out a single red rose. "You of all people know that with the right connections, stuff like that matters less."

I extend my hand to beckon him in, to accept the rose "You're so very right, Will. I do think you may be getting into the swing of things."

Chapter Ten

Most of the day, we are at lose ends until it is time to meet up. It won't do to be ready *too* early and have to sit around all day, but also fashionably late is impossible tonight. I spend some time doing my nails, just a very understated neutral pink. Nobody in the surveillance photos that Bits shared with us had their nails done in a remarkable manner.

I dither between wearing my jumpsuit to begin with, but decide it would be better if I wore a more normal outfit instead. I select one of my capsule dresses, so convenient, able to be balled up into a pocket and be effortlessly wearable in a pinch. One never knows when a quick change will be necessary. I consider my shoes, which can give so much away, and which Dolly and I have bickered about in the past. The weather is chilly enough that boots would not be out of place with my dress, and I lace on my velvet combat boots before spritzing on some perfume, just plain Chanel. It isn't supposed to rain.

The jumpsuit does fold up quite small, though still too large for a dress pocket, and I find a clutch that it will slide into that I'm not terribly attached to in case I must discard it.

Men have it easier, of course. Will is wearing a button down shirt and nondescript trousers, plain desert boots. He could be anybody walking down the street, ready to work or dine or gamble in a casino. Or put on a jumpsuit over that and move some art pieces about.

We walk a number of blocks, take a bus briefly, and then walk to the car park that is our meeting place. The mechanical arm is automatic; there isn't even a booth for an employee, and we walk around it and up to the third level without seeing or hearing another soul. I see Will casting wary glances at the cameras and lay a hand on his arm.

"Bits will have that in hand, darling," I say quietly.

"I'm just not used to that," he says. "And it's a little unbelievable, how much she manages at once."

"I do think that some of it is programs she runs? Perhaps housed, no, *hosted* in remote equipment? But I understand very little about all of that. She'll happily explain it to you, if you ask, but not exactly in what one might consider to be layman's terms."

"Maybe I will sometime."

Dolly and Perry are both smoking ecigarettes when we come around the corner, standing to the side of one of the vehicles and talking about it. Dolly notices us first, grins, and says, "Perry, I owe you a beer."

"Hey Bristol, Will," Perry says, also grinning.

"What was the bet?" I ask, though of course I already know.

"Dolly said you would be late," Garnet says, poking her head out of the other van. "Perry said no way, not tonight."

"What did you and Bits think?" I ask, smiling.

"We recused ourselves," Bits says from inside the van that Dolly and Perry are standing by.

"Cowards," Dolly says cheerfully.

"You have so little faith in me, Dolly?" I ask with a slight pout. She looks at me for a long moment, shadow of her grin lingering in the corners of her mouth.

"Bristles, I had every faith that you'd be exactly who I know you to be." I raise my eyebrows at her, and she turns away to the van. "Now come look at your duds."

"I will, thank you, though also I've made other arrangements."

"Now *I* owe *you* a beer," Perry says, tucking their ecigarette away.

"Beers for everybody," Bits says flatly, sliding out of the van, her headset hanging around her neck. She's already in a jumpsuit, wrists and legs cuffed, though the presumption is she will not be entering the casino. "Bristol, we talked about this."

"And I did nothing wrong," I say serenely. "I've brought my own jumpsuit here for your perusal, and if you think that it absolutely will not work, I'll use what Dolly and Perry procured for the group. The plan is still the plan."

"Sure it is," Dolly says. "Here, jumpsuits for everybody, then we'll look at Bristol's. How bad can it be, Bitsy?" The look Bits gives Dolly makes her laugh, and Perry's also smiling cautiously. Garnet is frowning slightly, perhaps taking her cue from me. Will is staying out of it, taking the offered jumpsuit and holding it up.

"These are good, they'll work," he says, in a positive, if slightly neutral, tone.

Dolly hands me the one she got from Germany, and then digs in her pocket. "Oh, I saw something at a rest stop that made me think of you."

"Oh, Dolly, that wasn't necessary," I say, and stop as she gives a vending machine capsule a shake and drops it in my hand. It's transparent, and I turn it enough that I can see it contains a pair of miniature black high heels, as if for a doll, with red soles. "Thank you, darling," I say with a little laugh.

"You see now?" She's grinning but studying me in an un-Dolly-like way.

"I do, yes." I open my clutch and shake out Amandine's jumpsuit. "The color is even shockingly alike, I'm actually surprised at that," I say, examining the two side by side.

Dolly takes it out of my hands and looks at it, then holds it up to the one Bits is wearing. "Huh. Gotta say, I was skeptical when Bitsy speculated what you might be up to. Not that you were up to something," she continues, seeing my face. "But how effective it'd be."

"And your judgment?"

"Guess we'll need to see it on, you might look *too* good," she says with a wink.

"I suppose that's a risk we must take," I say, pleased, feeling pre-party anticipation. I pointedly ignore Bits's eyeroll.

We get into our jumpsuits, and I present myself for judgment, confident enough that I shall meet Dolly's standards that I discreetly wiggle out of my dress and put it and my capsule of toy shoes into my pockets.

We reconvene, and Dolly rakes her eyes over all of us. To my eye, we all look serviceable. I'm really pleased with the fall of my jumpsuit over my boots, and how we all look together.

Dolly gets to me and stands there for a moment, also looking at my boots. I can't really read the expression on her face, as she brings her eyes up to mine and smirks. "Alright, I guess you pass muster."

"If you're certain," I say cautiously. How much time have I spent really *looking* at Dolly, concerned with how she thinks and feels? It is, of course, fleeting.

"Yeah, nobody's gonna notice. And you can have your little backup plan this way, go into the crowd or whatever if the jig seems up." We both smile, and she turns away. "Bitsy, you got eyes on the scene?"

"I've got eyes everywhere," Bits says, sounding mystified, or exhausted. "And Garnet's contact is in position."

Dolly checks the time on a watch that she wasn't wearing yesterday; another German vending machine purchase, one might assume. "Well. Guess we're ready to roll. Last chance if anybody's gonna tap out." She looks at Will, who looks steadily back at her. "Okay then. Everybody keep your eyes and ears open for trouble and communications. Bits'll paint the pathways in AR for you to get your sculptures to the van, so have your contacts in or glasses on."

She looks at me, pulls a glasses case from one of her pockets. "I know you're not normally about the AR life, but it simplifies things. I called Nicolai to get his opinion, so they won't be too tacky."

"Nicolai has good judgment," I say, taking the slim case. The glasses inside have rose gold frames, slightly smoke-tinted lenses. They would not look out of place with my clothing, in the casino, with its overbearing lights and machines and such. "Thank you. I ought to have thought of it and brought one of my pairs."

"Don't worry about it; we always look out for each other."
She winks and turns away, and I catch a glimpse of Bits's face,
just for a blink, before her expression returns to neutral. She
and Dolly have been, well, thick as thieves since we three got
together, and from what little Will told me, I'm now imagining
Bits in Dolly's ear, maybe even eyes, as she descended that sub
basement to retrieve him. Even before that, I'm imagining Dolly helping me after my drink was spiked at Rafe's ranch. Dolly
tackling me off the bridge in Macau. Bits and Dolly coming to
get me from Homeland after they'd sufficiently recovered from
our prior misadventure.

It isn't that I don't know I'm selfish. It's that it's been unnecessary for me to confront my selfishness in a meaningful way.
And now, as Will touches my elbow lightly to bring me out of
my reverie, is not the right time.

We clamber into the vans, Perry driving Garnet and Will,
Dolly driving Bits and I, making our unobtrusive way through
the evening streets to the casino. There's something knocking
about in the back, and I look over my shoulder into the cargo
area to see small, wheeled wooden platforms. "Are those—"

"The carts?" Dolly asks, grinning. "Yeah. And we, what's
Bitsy call it, we kitbashed the cover things that they do for the
statues. Shrouds? Whatever."

"Bits loves that word..." I say.

"It's a good word. So anyway, we've got extra ones for the
shuffle. It's like the cup game, you ever done that?"

"I have not." Not as such. So often, what we are doing socially is a cup game, n'est-ce pas?

"Shit, I can't believe I forgot," Dolly says suddenly.

"What? What's the matter?" I ask, Bits and others saying similar things in our ears.

"Bristol, you never been here before, right?"

"This casino? Heavens no, can you imagine."

"Obviously, yeah. And you're one who tends to stick out." Silence in our van and on the communications channel. Dolly has such a funny way with compliments, not even giving me a sidelong look as she delivers this latest one. "Anybody else? We should've asked this beforehand. Bitsy, you ever go here to watch the flashing lights?"

"Not this casino, no," Bits says cryptically.

"Good enough," Dolly says eventually, when nobody else confesses casinogoing. Over her shoulder, to Will, she says, "We're normally not this slapdash but this is a bigger team than normal and I was in another hemisphere 'til recently. As you know."

"...Yes," Will says cautiously.

"'Cause I wouldn't want you to feel bad, thinkin' you were always behind on catching up to us but we were just a rolling shitshow at all times. Which don't mean we don't wing it sometimes, but we're normally more prepared than this."

"Dolly, why are you making excuses?" I ask.

"I just don't want Mr. Secret Agent Man to think he only accidentally didn't catch us because we're a complete clown-show, but rather this is, uh, outside our usual scope." She really drawls the last part of her sentence, just to watch me squirm I'm sure.

"Honestly, Dolly," I say, but I can't help laughing.

"I didn't think that," Will says carefully. He has a stiffness around Dolly that is unlike any other demeanor I've ever seen him possess. Despite everything, or perhaps even because of everything, he's still extremely cautious of her. Perhaps less outright *frightened*. "I, and the Agency, are well aware of your capabilities, and have the deepest respect for them."

"Well thanks," Dolly says, grinning. "That's what we like to hear, right Bristles?"

"Well, yes," I say.

Chapter Eleven

The front of the casino is buzzy but not busy, and Dolly pulls through the parking lot and around to another entrance, with big bay doors and a ramp. "Guess this is us," Dolly says, putting the van in park and checking the mirrors. "Last chance, Will."

"I'm still in it," he says with quiet resoluteness.

"Garnet's cop?" Dolly asks.

"Doing his part," Bits says, and though Garnet is in the other van, I feel as though her relief is palpable.

There is a security guard rolling up the doors as we get out and Dolly and Will and Perry are removing the dollies. He gives us only a cursory glance, smoking a cigarette as he works. Dolly lights one of her own, and they share a mutual nod.

//Time starts now,// Bits says in our ears; she's remaining in the van to perform her hacking symphony, keeping track of so many things at a time it makes one's head spin, even if she did share some of the work out to this Nautical Deborah person. I've long since given up making any sense of the names that Bits's associates use.

"Roger that," Dolly and Will say almost at the same time, and I catch his rueful smile as she laughs. I slide on my glasses so that I can see the path and statues Bits has chosen for me.

This is one of the most delicious parts of a job, being at a location for reasons unknown to those around us, appearances altered, heady with risk, confident that everything will proceed according to plan. Dolly hands me a pair of absolutely dreadful looking work gloves as we all go off on our assignments.

Some of the larger and more intricate pieces are left on wheeled bases, which makes it easier to cowl them and move. It must preserve them better, if they needn't be handled every night, and I am immediately grateful for the gloves; they make it easier to manipulate the cowl, and the cart. It's surprising, or perhaps not, both how many casinogoers there still are this time of night, and also how invisible we are to them. I consider whether I would pay much attention to workers in jumpsuits in such a setting, and am unsure of my answer. Surely I would be curious about the cowled items, but then, there is still signage about regarding the art pieces. Most of it digital, presumably to change with each piece's location, but then there are also physical words on walls, naming the artist and exhibit.

I think about all of this as I find my first piece in the flashing lights and plush carpet of the slot machines floor, a wide-eyed and long tailed creature, and engage the first cowl. I expect to fumble with that at least a little, but it is a simple push button control, giving a very satisfying click when it engages. I wait until it is locked in place, and then make my trip to the van, a breathless exercise in 'surely somebody will soon stop me' but nobody stops me. Perry gets there at the same time, with their first statue, and we load both, using ratchet straps to secure them in the van before going back through the casino with our still-cowled carts for our next pieces. I must say, they are rather garish even for my tastes, but each piece of art isn't for every person.

Nobody stops any of us, throughout most of our endeavor. A security guard even helps me at one point, when one of my statues is a bit too tall for me to maneuver properly, a tremendous squid with tentacles counterbalancing it awkwardly, extending in odd directions from its platform.

"You lot are always doing that," is his only comment, chiding, amused.

"Merci," is all I say, tucking my chin in as though I am embarrassed.

The first wrinkle is when Garnet gets to one of the elevators and there's a velvet rope cordon and it says 'out of order.' The casino is quite large, of course, multiple stories, and we'd been using the elevators liberally. There are also rampways between floors, it would be so gauche to have stairs in such a newly built facility, but the art installation in general avoids the ramps and thus the general casino patrons, so of course we are doing as they do.

Garnet has been more anxious about this than we realized, though, coming onto our little network in a very small voice saying, //I can't use the elevator.//

//Here's the way to your nearest ramp,// Bits says almost immediately. If ever we're able to operate with her using a proper mainframe and immersion equipment, I'm certain we can do anything, based on her capabilities on the go.

//I know but—// Garnet cuts off, I think because she hears the whining tone in her voice, but perhaps also because patrons are near her. //I just didn't expect it,// she says. //It was fine when I came up.//

//How are we on security, Bitsy?// Dolly asks in a casual tone. //Garnet, gonna meet up with you, sit tight.//

//Normal chatter on their network, no alarm in their systems that I can see.//

//Well that's good,// Perry says cheerfully. //I just did a dropoff and I didn't see anything. All the guards were in normal spots.//

//Okay,// Garnet says dubiously.

//The thing is, kiddo, you just need to not look down,// Dolly says, and her voice comes through on her speaker and on Garnet's, so they really are very close.

//Okay,// Garnet says again.

I finish with my current statue, a small and manageable set of three birds, even with those horrid gloves. My next trip will be to leave an empty cowled cart in a similar location. This particular statue takes me past the cage where people exchange their cash or credit or chips, and I am aware of the casino employees' gaze when I am in view. They have seen this every night of the installation, so three weeks now, and thus it can't be too terribly interesting. It is difficult for me to keep it uninteresting, it isn't as though I don't know that about myself, but it is of utmost importance to keep steady, especially with our little team so far-flung throughout the building. I am not so childish that I would put us all in danger just now for the sake of some attention.

"There's a freight elevator," Dolly says as I come outside; she and Garnet are going back past me.

"Thanks," Garnet says, smiling desperately. "Sorry "

"Darling, no, you're fine." I glance from her anxious face to Dolly's mask of affable calm.

"C'mon, we'll do the next big one," Dolly says. "Bitsy, shuffle around our assignments." There is not much time left, I know, and not many items left. In the look Dolly gives me, I think she'll be glad to be done but is also not willing to stop early.

Outside, Perry takes my cart so that I can return quickly, and as they're loading my statue, I glance in at Bits, who must see me through one of the cameras as she raises her hand in a thumbs up without otherwise moving. Perhaps she's just going by the vibrations of the van. I return inside with an empty cart, bring it to its place, and then follow my course to my next statue. I only have one left, according to my glasses. A giraffe. I don't know how many the others have, Bits isn't cluttering my field of view with that much information. For instance, she has not put a counting-down clock in my AR, but she almost certainly has for Dolly. Curious, I once asked her to show me how she operates, and the resulting barrage of information, blissfully brief, was enough that I needed to have a glass of water and sit for a moment.

I cross the casino floor, straight through the slot machines and past the blackjack tables, to go up two levels and reach my final statue. It's in amongst some plants, tucked into a hallway next to a ramen vending machine, and something about all of that just makes it seem so nonsensical, and of course this type of whimsy is part of the point. Envision the giraffe, emerging from the foliage, selecting and eating ramen. The giraffe is large, hard for me to manage, but the cowl on the cart keeps it more balanced than the dreadful squid that I had problems with earlier.

I've just got it turned around and in motion back towards the main hall and the ramps, when Garnet comes onto our network. //My police friend just called me, he's had to let them go,// she says, sounding on the verge of tears. //I'm sorry, I know we're not done, but—//

//No time for sorry, everybody out,// Dolly says. //Sound off, locations? I'm at the vans with Bits.//

//I'm in the elevator down with Garnet,// Perry says.

//Right inside with my last dropoff,// Will says. He's been so quiet this entire time, and I haven't caught a single glimpse of him, not even when my assigned statue has required a second pair of hands. Certainly this is by design, Bits keeping us from distracting one another.

//I'm on the second floor,// I say. //How much time?//

//Not much,// Bits says, after a not-brief-enough pause. //Leave your statue. It's the only one we didn't get.//

I keep walking, casting my glance about for a place to arrange the giraffe. //Bristol, you gonna come out or what?// Dolly asks.

//Do I have the time?// I ask archly, locking the wheels and glancing about. Nobody is in view for the moment.

//Not if you don't try,// Dolly says, calm but tense, not quite gritting her teeth.

//I'll gain too much notice if I try,// I say. //I'll convert my jumpsuit and mingle with the crowd for a bit, and then make my exit when is natural and appropriate.//

//Bristol...// Will says, but he doesn't continue.

//You know I'm right. Go, so that Bits doesn't have to spread her resources even further covering your tracks.// Silence. //I'll be *fine*.//

//If you didn't have that fancy jumpsuit you wouldn't be so eager to do this,// Dolly says ruefully. //I should've guessed you'd have an angle.//

//I'm certain I don't know what you mean,// I say, slipping into a lady's room.

//We're going to take these to the buyer and I'm gonna grab a car and come back for you,// Dolly says. //Just sit tight some-place.//

//For heaven's sake, Dolly, it's a casino in Paris, you're acting like you're leaving me to walk through a wolf pack carrying steaks.//

//I'm not arguing with Dolly here,// Will says.

//Perhaps you should, darling, it would be good for you.//

I get into a stall and convert my jumpsuit, then go and redo my hair and makeup in the mirror, so that it matches my attire. I didn't wear earrings and there's nothing to be done about that, but the necklace I wore underneath the jumpsuit should suf-fice for adornment. I consider removing my earbuds, but they are *very* discreet, the newest model of tiny, bone-conducting sound, quite easy to cover up and forget about, and be able to hear one's surroundings as normal. It's amazing how far the technology has come, even in the few scant years since we start-ed working together. I do remove my glasses, though, and tuck them away into their case in my pocket.

//Bristol you can still get out a side door and take a taxi,// Bits says.

//I promise you that I will do nothing unusual or out of sorts and I will be perfectly safe in this brightly lit public area until Dolly or Will or both come to pick me up.//

//Are you doing this to see those art people's faces?// Bits asks.

//It is a rare opportunity,// I say. //But it didn't occur to me, and it's unlikely that I will see them very much at all.//

Chapter Twelve

I do have a moment, while getting chips, that I think the employees might recognize me from watching me go back and forth all night. They don't, though; they all seem preoccupied by a radio playing a football game, I think. The volume is turned down quite low.

The chips in my hands feel heavy, consequential, which is funny for something so trivial. It's only *money*, after all, which I will of course never do without, but also which I built up from nothing to begin with. I can lose everything I'm holding right now and it won't change my life one bit, and that's such a heady feeling, coming from seedy, run-down city apartments the way that I do.

Why do I keep *thinking* about that?

I walk out onto the casino floor and cast my glance around. I have no interest in the slot machines, nor poker, nor the dice games. I linger a moment with my eyes on the blackjack tables, but the rattle and chatter of the roulette wheel is what wins my attention.

This time of night, because it is late by now, there are only a few people around the table, watching the wheel, and their numbers, intently. Is the person who drops the little roulette ball still called a dealer? I've never thought about it before now.

I'm unsure of the etiquette of laying bets, and insinuate myself at the table to observe. "Rien ne va plus," the dealer says, and a moment later, the ball falls from its track into the wheel, and a moment after that, into a numbered slot. The bettors around the table make frustrated noises, and the dealer uses his croup to clear the bets.

The time for bets is indicated again, and this time, I put all of my chips on a red number, 27. The dealer's face remains impassive, but the bettor to my right gives a low whistle. "Are you sure?"

"Certain that it isn't your business," I say with a calm smile, glancing up at him. He's got sandy blonde hair and dark eyes, expression blurred by at least two drinks too many.

"Point to the lady," he says, and shifts one of his chips to my number as well, and with his movement, I get a whiff of very classic men's cologne, perhaps Bay Rum. "In case you're right."

"Maybe I'm lucky," I say.

None of the other bettors join us on that number, following their own whims, and the dealer sends the wheel spinning again, and the ball in the opposite direction. "Rien ne va plus," he says, and we all watch intently.

The revolutions slow, and the ball drops, and I smile and give a little laugh. My number is not where the ball has landed. This is quite the classy casino, and the dealer glances at me a moment, appraisingly, but with none of the apprehension one might see in a seedier establishment. The gentleman to my right lets out a strange exclamation, as though he's been hit with cold water and invigorated.

"You really don't know how much money you just lost, do you?" he asks, intent, smug, excited.

"Oh, I do," I say, airy, dismissive. I suppose I'm invigorated as well.

//Are you done playing, princess?// Dolly says in my ear, casual but with tension in her tone that I can discern.

"Thank you, I'll be on my way," I say to the dealer, and to Dolly, and turn from the table.

"Enjoy your evening," he says, by rote, but clearly baffled.

I'm six steps away from the roulette table when the other bettor catches up to me, like a little dog nipping at my heels. "I've never seen anything like that," he says.

"Perhaps you ought to get out more," I say, coy, dismissive. "Certainly far worse has to have happened here."

"I come here all the time. I've never seen you, though." He interposes himself in front of me, so I must stop walking and look at him. Perhaps not as drunk as I thought he was. I imagine he pictures himself in a romantic movie, using his attempt to woo the love interest before she walks out of his life forever. Unfortunately for him, I am not his love interest.

"Nor will you again," I say, growing impatient. "I had some time to waste this evening and now will be on my way."

He holds a hand out as I start to walk, but knows better than to touch me, apparently. Luckily. If I was wearing my usual heels, we would be the same height. "Please, let me—"

"I'm flattered by your regard, sir, but please step aside and allow me to leave," I say firmly, keeping our eye contact steady. "I am not available to you, and my ride is outside."

"People don't just say no to me," he says, not moving, but starting to waver.

"Perhaps they should, you need the practice at gracefully retiring." I take my next step, and he *does* move aside to let me pass. "Maybe you could hire somebody to train with."

He catches at my wrist, but misses and then stumbles. "I could hire you," he mumbles, perhaps thinking that he's speaking compellingly, urgently.

"You cannot." How tiresome. Even if I wasn't trying to make a graceful exit after a mostly-completed job, this would be so *boring*, so frustrating. I'm sure he thinks that he's rich enough or clever enough to be quite important, but I do not recognize him and do not share that sentiment based on my brief experience.

"I'll make it worth your—" he grabs at my wrist again, and this time, when he misses, it's because Dolly has appeared just to his side, her intent grin a clear threat, if one is smart enough to appreciate the intent of her posture.

"You got someplace to be, friend?" she asks in English, reminding me that all of this to now has been in French. Our interloper indeed understands her intent, and also English. Most non-Americans do speak multiple languages, after all; our little trio is unique in that we also do. I'm never certain what languages Dolly *does* speak, but part of her implicit threat just now is in her choice of language.

My would-be companion has snapped his gaze from me to Dolly and taken a half step back in some vestige of self-preservation. "I was having a private conversation," he says in English, stiffly, carefully.

"And I am bidding you good night before we must draw the attention of security," I say. "Return to your table, you seemed to be winning."

"But I—"

"Goodnight now," Dolly says, still grinning, stepping into the space that he left between us. He's confused by her grin, as people so often are, and she looks from him to me. "You ready?"

"Extremely," I say. I turn without returning my gaze to the man, and Dolly is just a step or so behind me as I walk towards the doors, and then out through them as they whisper open. No further protests ensue from the persistent stranger and while I would have disentangled myself quite well, Dolly's presence certainly sped it up.

There is some manner of low-slung sports car burbling at the curb when we get outside, and the doors chirp open when Dolly approaches. I slide into a seat and am surprised when Dolly lingers, shutting the door for me, before going to her side. I have a brief memory of her sliding across the hood, in Morocco. I didn't understand, I was just so despairing, so furious, that she would so easily render Will unto the wolves. Would I have sacrificed myself for him? Absolutely not. Dolly's actions were worth more than my anger.

"Dolly, I think we need to talk," I say, as we leave the casino parking lot.

"Uh oh," she says, in a somewhat comical tone, glancing at me. Her expression is intent, curious. "What's going on?"

"Well we haven't seen each other in nearly a year, there is that consideration." I pause, and a gulf of silence stretches out between us that she does not rescue me from, opting instead to drag on her ecigarette and crack a window. "And I suppose I'd like to talk about why," I say. "I know we don't always live together, and we've often separated after a job, but this time was—"

"Different," she says finally. "I guess what I'm interested in is when you realized it was different."

"I did say...I was awful to you, I'll admit that. I did say that I would never forgive you, and that simply isn't true, of course I've forgiven you." I pause again, and we drive on, too fast, I think, through the well-lit streets. "There was nothing to forgive." I'm *extremely* unused to fumbling for my words.

"Talked to Will, did you?" she asks, conveniently at a darker spot so I can only somewhat see her face in the dashboard lights, the headlights from a car that passes us. She seems casually interested, perhaps slightly amused. She knows I'm fumbling.

"I *did* talk to Will, and he was exceedingly uncomfortable, and said that there was only so much that he felt was his to tell."

"Did he now." She's thinking that over, and I let her. We've operated so often in the spaces between, societally, leveraged those to our advantage. I'm not sure how aware we've been of the spaces between us. "I think he can shape up to be a good one."

"I think so too," I say.

"That it?" She checks her mirrors, makes a turn without signaling.

"What? No, I feel as though we need to clear the air between us, don't you?"

"Do we? What, do you want me to slap you so we're even?"

"That isn't what I mean," I say stiffly, a little hurt.

"I don't know what you want, Bristles." She stops the car, I think abruptly, and puts it into park before looking at me.

We're next to a park that I never remember seeing before, lit warmly by an orange-y street lamp, and it rained at some point while we were in the casino, but is not raining right now.

"I want things to be the way they were," I say, a bit helplessly. "I want to address this strangeness between us, so that it doesn't become something bitter and awful."

"Just wishin' for something doesn't make it come true," Dolly says, a little ruefully.

"I've made quite a lot come true," I say. "Maybe this will too."

"Maybe."

"Will never wished in a fountain before," I blurt out. I hadn't meant to, and her raised eyebrows reflect that. "Coming back one night, we found one."

"What'd you wish for?" she asks.

"You can't ask somebody that!" I say, coyly.

"Oh that's right, it makes it not come true. Or is that birthday cake wishes? It's hard to keep 'em all straight." She drags on her ecigarette again, offers it to me. Normally, I would demur. Today, I take it. Perhaps it will steady my nerves, which I'm unused to thinking about. That surprises her too, but she watches without comment as I bring the device to my lips and draw in the vapor. Dolly tends to favor scents and flavors that are like baked goods, if she's using an edevice, and maybe this vanilla one is what made her think of birthday cake.

"I think most wishes are best kept between the person wishing and the means of wishing," I say. "Fountains and birthday cakes and falling stars."

"Dandelions," she says, taking the ecigarette back. "We kids used to make wishes on dandelion fluff."

"I've never done that," I say. While some greenery would struggle up through the cracked concrete of my childhood, it was somehow never dandelions. That seems impossible, but I don't remember dandelions.

"Well. Next time we see dandelions, if one of 'em's gone to seed, I'll make sure you get the wish," she says, and her smile is easier now. "Okay, we gotta go." She tucks the ecigarette into a jacket pocket and pushes open her door. I fumble with my door to follow her.

"The car was a short-term loan then?" I ask, as I catch up with her. She heads into the park, the entrance of which is a gate flanked by trees. There are other lights that I can see, sprinkled throughout, though I'm not certain it's necessarily supposed to be open just now.

"You might say that." We both laugh, and I feel relieved, steadier. "So what else do you want to know?"

"Beg pardon?"

"Well, you said Will said that he only felt comfortable telling you so much, or whatever. What else do you want to know?" Her eyes glint in the streetlight, and it's possible she's looking for an opportunity to brag, that's very Dolly, or it's possible that she wants me to leave things well enough alone, but she could just *say* so, that's even more Dolly.

"I'm not certain I know enough to know what to ask," I say. Dolly is walking quickly, and I'm just slightly behind her, to the side, as I don't know where we're going.

"Yeah, that's fair," she says, glancing at me, taking in my bare arms. "You warm enough in that?"

"I'm okay for now," I say. "But I will stand out very soon, if I don't already."

"Yeah. Perry's gonna pick us up on the other side of the park, it's fine."

"So soon?" I ask, disappointed. I'm not certain why I'm *surprised*, of course we have to meet back up with everybody, make sure the statues are dropped at the buyer and we receive our payment, all of the little post-job details.

"Will and Perry got the vans to the buyer's warehouse. The price they offered was market price plus a percentage I forget, that Bits accepted on Marquis' recommendation, sorry not to consult you. Then Will headed on home."

"No, that's fine, that's perfectly reasonable" I say, mystified. "And Bits?"

"In the wind on public transit, but also safe. Very politely not listenin' in on purpose, I imagine. We all stuck to the plan and got it done, other than that last part. Rarely has a job been so hitchless, which feels like jinxing things to say but..."

"Garnet, though." Our team has doubled so easily, which makes twice the people to keep track of.

"Perry's taking Garnet to her place before gettin' us. All noses counted,"

"Well." Dolly's right, it is rare for things to be so hitchless. We *did* have hitches, and they were minimal. "And you said we shouldn't do a casino job."

"And *you* said that it wasn't really a casino job," she says. She looks at me again and takes off her jacket. "Here, you're shivering."

"I'm fine," I say, but accept it. It *is* too cold for my converted jumpsuit's bared arms. If I made it back into a jumpsuit, I'd be warm enough, but that would mean refusing Dolly's generous offer. The jacket is a bit loose on me, and smells, comfortingly, of vanilla and tobacco and gun oil. I can't see Dolly's shirt quite well enough in this light, but that confirms in my mind that it's a newer, tactical fabric that specifically avoids reflecting light. Without her jacket, I can also see the slight bulk of her bullet-proof vest. "No dragonscale?"

"The shirt is, thought I'd double up this time, with the specter of casino security. Though that does remind me, those dragonscale camisoles you wear don't have coverage for shit, we need to work something else out for you."

".....oh indeed?" I ask after a moment, processing. "What's changed now that—" the very slight toot of a horn interrupts me, and Perry waves out the window of a car. What a strange little park, I wonder which one it is. I haven't seen any signs.

"That's our ride," Dolly says, and I look at her for a long moment.

"Please come to my flat," I say. "We'll have coffee."

"If you say so."

Chapter Thirteen

Perry chatters most of the way, about the car Dolly 'borrowed,' about the car we're riding in, which was also borrowed, about the vans and what we could've done differently with them, and I let Dolly engage them while I look out the window and think about the small fortune we've just made. About the risks we took in doing so, and how the thefts must have been only just now discovered by the real art team.

I listen idly for sirens but, realistically, are police going to rush across the city with all of the bells and whistles? The time for that was when we were still at the casino. Their investigatory time now is in gathering evidence at the scene, and trying to make sense of what Bits did to the video surveillance. I do wish I could see the looks on the art team's faces, which I presume Bits *does* have the privilege of. Perhaps she'll record it, but I would never ask to see.

"I'll see you when I see you, I guess," Perry says, pulling up at the curb just at my flat.

"We'll be in touch," Dolly says. "Be normal but lie low."

"This isn't my first job," Perry says, defensive but also positively vibrating with excitement. I feel the social pull for a moment, Dolly's impulse to go with our young colleague, that they

103

might both blow off some steam, as it were, but under Dolly's discreet tutelage.

"Yeah, I know. Still." Dolly gets out of the car, closes the door firmly, knocks twice on the roof. We watch Perry drive away. "They're desperate to get it right," she says.

"Yes, and that outweighs their need to brag," I say, opening the door. Dolly follows behind me, not too close. Will left the light on the landing on, and I expect him to be waiting for us, but he isn't in evidence and the door to his room is closed.

"Must've crashed, who can blame him," Dolly says, but her smile says she can blame him, all right.

"Make yourself at home, I'm going to get changed," I say, sliding her jacket off and handing it back to her.

"You're just tickled pink that your trick jumpsuit worked," she says to my back, a laugh in her voice.

I give a little laugh. "Why, of course I am." What to wear, though, when sitting around with Dolly after having a job and a fragment of a heart to heart? I remove my jewelry and hairpins and drop all that in a tray on my dressing table, then pull my capsule dress out of the jumpsuit pocket and shake it out before returning it to a hanger. I return the jumpsuit dress to jumpsuit form and hang that up as well. I take the capsule of miniature designer shoes from the jumpsuit pocket and look at them again, smiling. What a funny little thing. I set that in my jewelry tray as well, for now, before surveying my closet. After considering perhaps a bit too long, but honestly Dolly would expect nothing less, I select a pair of soft linen palazzo pants, a camisole with lace edging, and a long chunky cardigan to go over that. I slip into ballet flats and go to find Dolly.

At one point while getting changed, I did hear a cork, and so I know that I can find her in the little library. She's standing at an angle, looking down at the rainy street, but just before I come in, she's already turning. There's a glass with two fingers of whiskey in it for her, but next to that is a stemless flute, bubbles floating to the surface from a disintegrating sugar cube. A fresh lemon twist is draped over the rim, sharp scent in the air.

"Champagne cocktail is your drink, right?" she asks, reaching to hand it to me.

"It is, thank you," I say, surprised that I am charmed, that Dolly would know or have noticed. I have a sip, remembering the bracingly sour drink that Will made me the other night, when I asked him to make me something nice.What a difference. "You're always such a deft hand with drinks," I say. Poor Will.

"Another life," she says, smiling crookedly.

"After the super soldiery but before I found you at that dreadful bar?"

"Yeah, and some in-betweens too. Why don't we do that next?"

"Do what next?" I ask, allowing myself to frown just slightly. "Go to a dreadful bar?"

"No, no, our next job should be a bar heist. Wouldn't that be funny, just takin' a wholeass building somewhere? Maybe we could put it on a barge and take it out to Bitsy's hacker friends. Nautical Deborah? I'm shocked you didn't ask about that."

"I know better than to inquire regarding the names hackers choose for themselves," I say. "Bits is somewhat plainly named for her profession, wouldn't you say?"

"Ain't that the truth," she says, sipping at the whiskey. I wonder which of Will's collection she'd decided to sample. "I know you said coffee, but I figured a drink would hit the spot."

"Besides the dangers of letting you loose in my kitchen. I'm not certain what would be left for breakfast." We laugh together, and that's very nice as well. I settle into a chair, tuck my legs up beneath me. "Dolly darling, I'm so glad you're here. I don't know what I would've done if you'd sent me away when I came to you in Hong Kong."

"Cried a lot," she says affably, finishing the whiskey with a toss. Not such that she'd like to savor it, then. "Not done the job, anyway."

"Hmm, I suppose we'll never know," I say. *Would* I have sought out another hacker, to replace Bits? I didn't find her in the first place; Dolly did.

"Nah, I know." She pours herself another whiskey. It isn't the same bottle Will used to steady himself, the label is a different color. She sighs, as though preparing herself. "Anyway, you still wanted to talk?"

I'd honestly almost forgotten, so settled in and chatting the way we were. "I do, but I'm at a loss. I can hardly ask a catalog of your injuries, going to extract Will in the manner that you did. Also, what do you *mean* my dragonscale doesn't cover very much, and also how could it possibly? You're familiar with what a camisole is."

"Yeah I'm familiar with what a camisole is and now I'm conversant with what it fuckin' feels like to be shot when wearing one." I stare at her, perhaps even gape, all of my artifice shocked away. I'm grateful I chose this cardigan to wear, as I'm sure my arms are just all gooseflesh. "I took one of your dragonscale camisoles and a dress in a can when I went to get to Will, since I had to get through like, three overlapping party situations in a hotel lobby before the secret door to the secret sub-basement."

"Oh, Dolly," I say, because I *haven't* been shot while wearing a dragonscale camisole, or at all actually, for all of the protective wear that Dolly insists on we three having for every job. I'm not certain Bits has either. Only Dolly. "Oh, Dolly," I say again, and she puts her hand up before I can continue. Her real hand, not her replacement.

"Nah, Bristles, it's okay, I lived through it. One was in the guts, which it *did* stop, it just sucked worse than a vest or a jacket, but the other one was through the shoulder, which isn't covered at all by the little strappy bits at all. So unless you're gonna Joan of Arc it or something with some kind of haute couture pauldrons, find a designer to make you an actual bulletproof jacket that you're actually willing to wear, huh?"

"I might have just the designer in mind," I say. "The woman who made my jumpsuit might be willing to work with me on bespoke products."

"Perfect, good, thank you."

We're quiet for a moment, and I remember my glass. The sugar has all but dissolved by this point, which is part of the pleasure of the champagne cocktail for me. I am not always able to have it with a sugar cube when I ask for it at a bar, and they substitute simple syrup without warning, which must seem the same to them, depending on the quality of bartender, but it is not to me.

"Will is grateful that you saved his life," I say eventually.

"I know," she says, and then laughs at my scandalized look. "He *told* me. There, at the time. I didn't expect it wore off." She finishes her newest whiskey and then says, "I guess he could be forgiven for thinkin' I wouldn't remember, though, on account of the head trauma and blood loss."

"Perhaps," I say faintly. I set down my drink on the table next to me, still fizzing just a bit. "I am also grateful that you saved his life," I say. "I...my actions were quite unlike everything I have done to bring myself to that point, and then also to this one."

"The ice princess was feelin' something, is all," Dolly says. "I already told you that I don't need you to say sorry."

"What, then?"

She shrugs. "You're the one who said we needed to talk." But she's watching me, no matter how casual her posture.

"Because we never *do*. And because I didn't know what *happened*, to you or to Will. And because I didn't know why you went away, and stayed away for so long. And then I find out you got married and you didn't tell me."

"If I had told you, you would've wanted to plan the wedding, and I'd already been party to that once."

"That was a *fake* wedding!" I say in protest.

"For you. Your friend sure got married for real." She stops, her head cocked, listening. I listen too, but I know her ears are better than mine. Enhanced to be, perhaps. Another question I shall never ask. "Which begs the question, what're you gonna do with Will now that you got to keep him?"

"Pardon?" I thought I heard Will in his rooms, perhaps that's what she was paying attention to. Or perhaps it was somebody passing on the street.

"You're awfully cozy here, and I've never even seen you give somebody a second date," she says, watching my face again. "Not that it makes a difference. I'm just askin', since it'll get real awkward if you two break up but he's still pulling jobs with us."

"This was only his first involvement," I say. I feel such relief, that she said *us*. Jobs with us. "I have...oh it sounds wicked, but I have somewhat been keeping him like a house pet to this point. He's been adjusting to what this sudden, structureless life of luxury means, coming from the agency, and his upbringing. Also how he feels after being deprogrammed. He hadn't quite realized the extent of how that would make him feel."

"Yeah, the emotional partitioning isn't something that they tell the non-soldiers very much about," she says. "Still applies to them, but I think they get to feel a little more than they let us. But depending on who you are, it's overwhelming when that wall comes down." She's watching my face as she says that, more intently than normal, and catches some change. "Bits told you that part, then. Somebody did."

"That you were reactivated before going down to retrieve Will, yes," I say.

"Not gonna ask about that?" Finally, she sits, in the chair next to mine.

"You were just now nagging me regarding my protective equipment." She cocks her head. "For that particular operation, reactivating your programming was another layer of protection."

She laughs, startling me but also, somehow, making me relax. I hadn't realized quite how tense I'd become. I hadn't realized I could lose my sense of that. "Sometimes you really get me, Bristles," she says.

"I should hope so," I say. "We've done this for some time now, we know some things about one another."

"A thing or two," she agrees. "In some cases, we've maintained the mystery."

"There has to be *some* mystery left to remain, darling," I say. "And, I'm very glad that you agreed to talk to me, so we could regain our footing."

"Yeah, me too," she says. She finishes her whiskey, gets up with her glass. "You done?" She gestures.

"Nearly." I finish the last little bit, the sweetest part.

"You dripped some," Dolly says, brushing her thumb across my chin, natural as you please.

"Thank you," I say softly, my face tipped up to hers, and that's when she leans down and kisses me.

She tastes smokey from the whiskey and like vanilla, and there's a little rough spot on her lower lip. I hear the thud of her whiskey glass on the plush carpet as she puts her hands in my hair, and while I kissed her once under the mistletoe for a lark, that was a friendly peck. This is entirely different.

I've been a fool about Dolly, deliberately, both because we have to work together and also because men have been my romantic interest, but kept at an arm's length. Everybody, always, kept at an arm's length. Part of my protective equipment.

But I've never been good at kissing and thinking at the same time and those thoughts mostly fade to a background buzz, and then Dolly has pulled back away again, retrieved her glass from the floor and taken mine. "I'll take care of these," she says, her voice soft but rough-edged.

"Leave them," I say, catching at her hand, but she's already out of reach again.

"Don't worry about it, Bristol," she says, and disappears down the hall. I sit a moment with the memory of her lips on mine, in that cozy room, and then I follow her down the hall.

She's devilishly quick with washing up, and she's already drying her hands by the time I'm in the tiny kitchen with her. She didn't turn any lights on, but enough light comes through the window from the streetlights.

"Dolly, I would have—"

"I know," she says. "But I try to be a good guest and act like I'm housebroken, every once in a while. Keeps you guessing."

"Yes, but..."

She gives me an easy grin, brushes past me to take her jacket off of our rack by the entryway. "I'm gonna get going. But we'll all be in touch, I'm sure."

"*Dolly*," I protest, but I stop when she looks at me.

"What?"

I don't fully know the implications of what I mean, but I say, "Stay."

She looks at me for a long time, or just a heartbeat. "Sorry, princess," she says, eyes full of possibility and regret. And then she slips out.

Chapter Fourteen

I n the days that follow, we as a group have no contact with one another. That's preferable, in fact, if a job has gone well, and has served us well in the past. It's all over the news, of course, that those statues were stolen, only one left behind. There's much speculation about that one, to great hilarity, I think. Bits and Dolly must be having a ball over it, and the pictures are quite comical, of that giraffe in situ.

I keep looking at that giraffe, thinking of how close I was to completing the full sweep. They've left it there, both as evidence mais oui and also artistic statement. All the animals were endangered or extinct.

G arnet, Will, and I have lunch with Marquis. We carefully do not discuss the job, we wouldn't have anyway, especially not with Marquis. I'll confess to being quite distracted by my daydreams, such that my distance is noted without very much time having passed.

"Bristol, do you need anything?" Garnet asks, a frown wrinkling her brow. Will's expression of schooled blankness is one that I know well, and Marquis is simply amused.

"I'm so sorry, darlings, I've been far away from you." I smile, sip my sparkling water to regroup. "What were we talking about?"

"The latest news out of the election," Garnet says.

"You were not, and I don't even need to ask what election to know that," I say, laughing. "You don't need to punish me by threatening to talk politics."

"That's a relief, because I'd much rather talk about the crime that these patterns are that everybody suddenly thinks we're going to wear on *harem pants* in the spring," Marquis says, setting their phone on the table and tapping it to make the image project.

"Just horrifying," I agree, watching the model rotate. "Do we know the justification?"

"Not as such," Marquis says. "I suppose once we find the first person who started doing it, that will be something well done that makes sense. At this point, we're looking at the end result of a game of telephone."

"I'd agree," I say. "While it wouldn't be *impossible* to make these work..."

"Oh Bristol," Marquis says, clicking their tongue in disappointment, and Garnet laughs.

"I'm sorry, Bristol, I agree with Marquis."

"An unforeseen betrayal!" I turn to Will in appeal. "Tell them, Will darling."

"I, uh, didn't know those were called harem pants until today," Will says with a helpless shrug.

"My goodness, the next thing you're going to tell me is that you're color blind."

"No, I'm not. My brother is, though. Red green." He clears his throat and takes a drink; he's never mentioned a brother to me. He makes every effort to never mention his family at all, as a matter of fact. Every personal story he's told was about himself, and friends. Very occasionally colleagues. As I also never mention family, and given the clandestine nature of our existence, while I've been curious, I haven't pushed.

"Will shouldn't have to worry about it, after all," Garnet says soothingly. "He isn't the expert, you are."

"Also very true," I say.

"Glad to be off the hook." Will flags the server for our check, and his phone chimes in response. "I just wear what Bristol tells me, and tell her that she looks nice." He glances at me. "To be clear, I've never not seen her look nice."

"Nor will you," Marquis says. "Bristol doesn't have a state of being which would be considered not looking nice."

"It's very hard work," I say, smiling.

"I don't look nearly as good at Bristol at all times, and can vouch for just how hard it is," Garnet says.

"You sell yourself short," Marquis says. "Bristol's simply been honing this knife longer than you."

"You sound like Dolly," I say, a bit curiously.

"Perhaps. Who can say." We all stand and get our coats and scarves, exchange our kisses and embraces and go on our separate ways.

"That was nice," I say to Will in the car, and he makes a noise of assent.

"Marquis knows how to put somebody at ease." He pauses long enough that I think that is his full statement, and then he says, "All three of you do, actually. It makes things a little weird sometimes."

"Oh indeed?" I ask. I'm aware of what he means, I think, but I'm curious.

"I kind of feel like a mouse in a roomful of cats, and that isn't a way I ever felt in a roomful of people with guns." He looks at me, gives a short, self deprecating laugh. "Don't worry about it, it's how things are."

"Well darling of *course* I have to worry about it! Do you feel that way when it's just you and I?"

"Mostly, it's when we're all in a group," he says carefully.

"So sometimes it *is* when it is just you and I." My tone is also careful, especially as he's just called attention to my social positioning proclivities.

"I didn't mean to upset you," he says, looking at me with genuine care and concern.

"You haven't upset me, other than to think you haven't been able to feel comfortable in your own *home*, such as it is." I think the Paris flat is very cozy, actually, but that is neither here nor there. "Will, it's been nearly a year."

"I said sometimes. It isn't all the time."

"Which is one reason you wouldn't have told me, of course, because how could one bring up that topic?" I smile at him reassuringly, search his eyes for the calculation of whether the smile is genuine. I see it now, of course, and I'd seen it before, of course, but left it up to him to voice. So much of his newly-freed time has been in discomfort, and I thought it best not to try and manage that every step of the way. There is also the stark reality that there is only so nurturing that I am, as a person. Will had to decide for himself who he was, in the absence of the Agency, and his programming.

It's interesting, just how different his newly-freed experience was from when Dolly was. She grew a bit more emotional, of course, as she suddenly was able to process far more emotions, but perhaps there is just something to be said for the reckless confidence she has always possessed, and how that has carried her through, programming or no. Will has always been a more cautious creature, though I myself would not have called him a *mouse*. Nor myself a cat, I suppose.

"I'm sorry that it took me so long to say anything," Will is saying.

"You had to process your thoughts and feelings. It's best to do these things in your time." Besides the fact that neither I, nor Marquis, nor Garnet, is likely to be able to change based on Will's complaint or discomfort.

"I appreciate that. I probably wouldn't know if you were mad, but I don't think you are."

I laugh, lean over to give him a peck on the cheek. "I'm not mad, no."

"Okay, good."

We pull up at the flat and I wait on the sidewalk while Will pays the driver; he likes tipping in cash, which I think tends to be appreciated. I get a sense that somebody is approaching, and look up to see Dolly standing by our door, her hands in her pockets.

"Bad time?" she asks, squinting a little at the angle of the sun.

"No, no, we've just come back from lunch." I look at her, thinking of how she kissed me. How could I not? "What's the matter?"

"I wanted to get out of Bitsy's hair and you're who I know here, and I realized I've never been up the Eiffel Tower and I figured you probably also haven't 'cause it's such a tourist thing to do."

"It does have a somewhat well-regarded restaurant," I say, as Will closes the car door and I hear his pause as he turns to walk towards me.

"But you haven't been to it."

"I haven't, no." I glance at Will, who is looking from me to Dolly, unsure of the footing here.

"Tourist shit is fun, that's how it gets that way. Come on." Dolly grins at me; her complete disregard of Will should probably be insulting, but I think he is relieved. They've seemed more comfortable with one another since she came to Paris, his plain fear of her tempered, or tamped down, but he would still prefer not to be in her company.

"You don't mind, do you darling?"

"What, if you go do, uh, tourist shit with Dolly? No, go ahead, it might be fun."

"If she lets it be," Dolly says, grinning.

"I know how to have *fun*!" I protest.

"Sure you do. I even took pity on you, get in the car."

"What?" I turn, and another hired car has replaced the one that Will and I just arrived in.

"I couldn't see you wanting to walk there from here, and then go up it." She holds the door for me, then slides in after. "At least, not on a full stomach."

"You're so thoughtful." She's correct, of course. It isn't as though I stuffed myself silly at lunch, which she would likely also know, but the further car ride through the city is most welcome. I peer out the window at the people we pass, and when I glance at Dolly, she's doing the same. We have wildly disparate goals, I presume; she assesses threats for fun and I assess outfits and postures, and the relationships that I glimpse.

At the tower, she stands at the base and looks straight up for a minute, like she's really taking it in and living in the moment. I watch her face curiously; I've seen Dolly perform such violence and so naturally, and also do such joyful, guileless things as this. If I were to strike a pose, looking up at the Eiffel Tower, I would be considering the angles of viewers, how to arrange my face, my shoulders, my hands. I'm confident that Dolly does not do that. She is perhaps the least concerned of anybody I have ever met with what people think of her, other than Bits, of course.

Then she looks at me. "Let's go."

"Lead the way," I say, smiling.

She walks past the delightfully retro ticket booth in the esplanade at the base, or maybe it's the original ticket booth, carefully maintained over the centuries. That is something that I love about Paris, so much of here is old, original, *cared for.* Once we're past, I realize that though she nodded to the person in the booth, no money or information seems to have changed hands.

"Dolly?" I ask, as she gets to the stairs in one of the legs. "Are we—?

"Going to see Paris as few ever do? Yeah."

"Dolly there are *so many* stairs," I say, looking up.

"The finest things in life aren't always easy," she says, as though I don't already know.

The stairs are solid metal decking, not mesh, and so I needn't worry about catching my heels in the gaps, at least. It doesn't occur to me to count the steps until I'm out of breath and my legs are burning and we're still not up to the first floor yet. "Dolly," I gasp at one point, and somehow she hears me. She pauses to wait, leaning against a railing and pulling out her ecigarette, which might be the most maddening part of all of this.

"You're in pretty good shape but you never did wanna drill," Dolly says, when I get close enough to hear a normal tone of voice.

"Sometimes you do give the strangest compliments, darling," I say, pausing a few steps down from her. The breeze is nice, and I close my eyes briefly as I face it.

"Yeah, it's one of my better qualities," she says. "Come on, not much further, and I'll buy you a drink." I scoff, and she laughs, and we keep going.

She again doesn't wait for me, and disappears at the top as I somewhat grimly keep climbing. I've long known that Dolly and I enjoy different amusements, but also I do think that this excursion is her trying to do something she thinks I'll enjoy. Somehow. It's true that I've avoided the tower because of how tourist-laden it is, but also it's exactly the sort of storied and ostentatious thing that I enjoy. And the silver lining of having taken the stairs is that we haven't seen anybody else.

I reach the landing, finally, and take a moment to physically and mentally straighten myself before stepping onto the main floor. There are shops here, and restaurants. A moment later, Dolly appears with a glass bottle of mineral water. "When you said a drink..."

"Yeah sorry, I meant to hydrate," she says, not looking sorry at all. "I'll buy you a real drink at the top."

I take a drink from the bottle, meaning to have a few sips, but instead I keep going until half of it is drained. "The top," I repeat.

"You didn't figure we were going to stop at the first floor?" She waits, and I drink the rest of the water. "The view's great, though, have a look and I'll put that in recycling."

"Thank you, darling" I say, and move to a railing, near to one of the shiny chrome telescopes that dot the perimeter. There are people here, it isn't as though she mysteriously was able to clear the location for us, but we seem to have gotten lucky and it isn't a very crowded day. I feel as though this would not be very enjoyable at all, were we jostling elbows with numerous strangers.

The view is lovely. Even at just the first floor, higher than my flat, which overlooks the street and the building across from it. It is a somewhat cloudy day, though not gloomy.

My respite is all too short, however. Dolly reappears at my side, also gazing out for a moment, as collected as if we'd just walked down a flat block at a leisurely pace. I consider if I've ever heard her out of breath, actually; yes, in Macau, after she tackled me off that bridge into the water. Did she know I could swim, before that moment? I've never asked her.

"You ready?"

"I suppose," I say, smiling as serenely as I know how.

The second floor feels much easier to reach, comparatively. Perhaps I've transcended wallowing in the difficulty of it, and hit my stride. Or perhaps I'm simply wrong, I have not been keeping time, though I cannot speak for whether Dolly is. Certainly there seem to be a similar number of steps, which I once again forget to count.

On the second floor, the crowd is thinner and the view that much more breathtaking, and I gaze out at it as I open my coat, too warm to leave it closed despite the chill in the air. Dolly is at first nowhere to be found, or rather, when I don't find her at first glance I simply pick a vantage and wait once again. Taking pity on my aching feet, I slip off my heels. It is perhaps too cold to stand here in my stocking feet, but for the moment, I don't mind.

She appears at my elbow before I can decide to remove the folding flats from my purse, a twinkle in her eye. "You ready?" she asks again.

I glance from her to the summit still above us. "I've heard only the lift is open to the summit," I say hopefully.

"Yeah, normally. But I know a guy." She laughs when she sees my face. "They replaced the spiral staircase way back when, it's totally safe. Probably even boring."

"Oh yes, heaven forbid we escape the mortal peril of a spiral staircase and wavery railing at three hundred meters."

"Gotta live a little, Bristles," Dolly says, and I follow her over to the gated stairs, past the entrance to the elevator. Marquis had a date here, just to a restaurant on the first floor, and said that the elevator was delightfully coggy, reminiscent of a more mechanical age that certainly none of *us* was alive to experience. Nobody stops us as Dolly opens the gate and we pass through.

The final ascent does have me feeling nervy, but the stairs are more than sturdy. We emerge to take in the city through the grid of protective wire around the summit, and I all but gasp to see Paris at our feet and to the horizon all around us.

The wind is sharper here, and I'm not certain it's possible to feel the tower's slight sway, I feel as though I do. "Oh, Dolly," I say softly.

"I knew you'd like it," she says, and when I look at her, I expect to see that grin on her face. Instead, I find a much softer smile.

"You know me so well," I say.

"Hmm, yeah, at least a little. I also figured you'd wanna stop in at the champagne bar, assuming they don't turn me away based on the dress code." I laugh with her, but I do eye her critically; she's dressed pretty typically for her, black cargo pants, black leather jacket that I'm certain is reinforced and bulletproof, a t-shirt with a logo that I can't quite make out.

"If they do, perhaps your 'know a guy' status will allow us to simply have our glasses out here." I glance about. "We seem to have a private viewing for the moment, after all."

"Back in a sec."

I slip my shoes back on and glance toward the champagne bar, which looks as though it's meant to echo the retro quaintness of the ticket booth in the esplanade. I believe it's much more recent than that. I know that there is also the architect's office, rendered into a museum, but I'm not terribly interested in that and I presume Dolly is also not. Though it's a surprise, sometimes, what she's interested in.

She returns, champagne-less. "They were impervious to your wiles?" I ask.

"It's not a go-in kinda place, so we can just sidle up and order the bubbly to sip while lookin' at Paris from the tippy-top."

"Well that's very nice," I say. I wonder if sometimes Dolly doesn't know what to talk about, when the language being used isn't one of violence.

At the champagne bar, the attendant is waiting with a carefully neutral look on their face, but from their change of posture, I can tell that they were betting with themselves who Dolly's companion might be, and I was not it. We make quite a pair, I suppose, she as she is and myself in a dress and high heels, a long wool coat.

"Look, they got pink champagne," Dolly says. "You want that?"

"That would be lovely," I say, amused and charmed to let Dolly make our champagne selections. What does she know of champagne, I wonder? Other than it must come from the proper region, mais oui.

I listen to her order, and pay, watching the attendant's face. Paris can be hard on the non-native speakers, even I have run into people a bit more relentless than they should have been, but I suppose in the most touristy of places, some standards must be relaxed. "My French is awful," she says cheerfully, as she turns and hands me my glass. "My Spanish messes it up, I don't ever have a problem there."

"I think that your demeanor also appeals well to the Spanish," I say. I am prepared to endure a subpar glass of champagne for the sake of having indulged Dolly, but it is quite good, actually. And, honestly, even champagne that is subpar does tend to still be good. There is a more specific threshold of quality that applies to it.

"Yeah, probably. They like my swagger."

I laugh. "Machismo, don't they call it?"

"I dunno, is it still machismo for a woman?"

"Perhaps not." We sip our champagne and look out over the city.

"This might've been nicer at night, but colder, so..." She says, trailing off.

"No, this is wonderful, Dolly, truly. I'm touched you even thought to do it."

"Yeah, well." She shrugs, but she's smiling. We drink our champagne and look out at Paris and sway, or don't sway, in the wind. When we've finished, she says, "You want another one?"

"Oh...well why not," I say, and she takes our glasses. The hard glitter of the sun off the Seine makes me think of diamonds, of course, which makes me once again think of the art pieces we stole, and the singular one that we missed. I don't realize quite how lost in thought I am when Dolly returns, as I very naturally take the glass of champagne, but at some point she jostles me a little bit.

"Bristles, you listening?"

I realize no, no I haven't been, I didn't realize that she was talking. I turn to her, and find myself once again looking deeply into her eyes, and as I am quite sure we're alone, I say, "Dolly, I want to go back and steal the last statue."

Her eyebrows shoot up, and she laughs loudly enough that I think all of Paris must hear her. "Of course you do," she says, shaking her head. "Guess we gotta figure that out."

Chapter Fifteen

We meet at a little out of the way cafe, just we three, Bits and Dolly and I. Two glasses of champagne are hardly enough to affect me much at all, other than a light sort of heightened mood. An awareness of the boundless possibilities of the world. Bits is perhaps not surprised that Dolly demanded her presence, as Dolly is wont to do exactly that, which is how I ended up climbing the Eiffel Tower with her to begin with. Bits is exceedingly surprised to find that I think we ought to do another job. More fully complete the first job.

"Well we can't pull the same trick twice," she says eventually.

"Do you think we can do it at all?" Dolly asks. "I mean we can do it, obviously, but like, in a nice way, without hails of bullets. Minimal bloodshed."

"It was one of the big ones," Bits mutters. "You read the papers right? There are pictures of where Bristol left it, which is where they left it too."

"Why would I read the papers." Dolly sits back as the waitress sets a *burger* in front of her, of all things, which must be why we came to this establishment in particular. A burger in Paris, indeed.

"Of course, this might be exactly what they want," I say. "For us to return to the scene of the crime."

"So you didn't read the papers either," Bits says.

"Why would I read the papers?" I ask in wide-eyed innocence. "I looked at the pictures."

Bits refills her coffee and dumps sugar into it. I am unable to tell if her unfocused expression is because she's looking something up online with whatever dreadful thing she had implanted, or if she just genuinely doesn't know what to say to me. Us. Dolly waits for her, though, chomping enthusiastically into her burger. She winks at me and nudges her basket of pommes frites in my direction, and I roll my eyes, and sigh, and take a few. They are very good, I think, shockingly good in fact. She leaves the basket between us.

"Okay, so, one angle that the article writer took, or maybe even the police in charge of investigating, they left it kind of unclear, is that the theft of the statues is part of the installation."

"They *what?*" Dolly and I exclaim at the same time. Bits blinks at us. I can see calculations on her face, but am at a loss as to what answer she arrives at.

"They kind of acted like it was all part of the show."

"That's honestly rather amazing, wouldn't you say?" I say after a moment, eating more of Dolly's fries. "Audacious, even. They've lost so much money—"

"That's just it, the money isn't the point, for them," Bits says. "Which seemed to me, and I looked this up, that the main artist is independently wealthy anyway. His parents died yachting or something and he's been trying to burn through a certain amount of the trust fund every year. Last year, he gave a ton of money to the people who run the trains in Madagascar."

"Bitsy, sometimes I got no idea what you're saying to me, and it's one of my favorite things about you," Dolly says, finishing her burger and wiping her hands. "Okay so what, we just walk in and take it and it won't matter, because the artist says that everything is fucking dying anyway?"

"That's kind of what the article says," Bits says after a moment, I presume once she's read it again. "Which feels like a trap."

"It does," Dolly agrees. She's looking around like she can't decide what to eat next. I nudge the basket back over to her, and she shrugs and starts eating fries again.

"Have you heard from Garnet whether her policeman has been in touch?" I ask.

"I know he hasn't, but no, I haven't heard from her. We're supposed to be following our usual habits."

"Which I have been," I say. "She didn't mention at lunch, of course."

"Lunch today," Bits says, not entirely a question.

"Yes lunch today, as if you didn't know already, Bits darling. You don't need to pretend, it's all right. We are honest with one another, if you'll recall."

"Sure we are," Dolly says easily. "Bits just loses track of the days, is all."

Genuinely, she does, while being acutely aware of so much other data at all times. It's unfair, all that we ask of her so much of the time. But also with her capabilities, who *knows* what she would be up to otherwise. How much she is already up to otherwise; Dolly has made mention that our little jobs are not such that Bit's attention needs full engagement for much of it. When we are actively performing, of course, we receive the full brunt of her laser focus, but with all our idle time, Bits could be dragging down distant governments if she wanted to, and we would be none the wiser.

Bits doesn't follow up with whatever her implication was, though. Instead, she says, flatly, "Are we seriously considering this." She is looking at Dolly, and thus I look at Dolly, who grins and shrugs.

"Aren't we?"

Bits looks from Dolly, to me, and sighs. "How do you want to run it?"

"The freight elevator is fairly closeby, that was where I was going to take it," I say. "Perhaps we could enter that way, without engaging with the casino floor, just scoop the statue up and be out again."

"Yeah maybe," Bits says dubiously. She drinks her coffee, looking off to the side, and Dolly lightly drums her fingertips on the table. I simply compose my expression and wait. Dolly flags the waitress at one point to get another pot of coffee, in order to keep Bits supplied.

Will sends me a message at one point, //Will you be back for supper or should I just fend for myself?//

//I'm afraid you're fending for yourself tonight, darling,// I reply. //Do please enjoy all the dreadful American sports television you desire.//

//I'll miss you.// he responds.

//And I'll miss you.// He is truly very sweet, and it isn't as though I've tired of him already, exactly, but being together again with Bits and Dolly, natural as can be, has made him fade a bit from my immediate thoughts.

"I do think we can do it," Dolly says to me in a confidential tone. "What can they do right? In public, in a building full of civilians? We've pulled that before, and more."

"I can still hear you, you know I can still hear you," Bits says.

"You always say that, but sometimes you're really just unreachable. I guess that's more when you're headset up, to be fair."

Bits blinks, looks at the both of us while reaching for her coffee. "Thank you."

"Well what's the good word, Bitsy?"

"We're going to need some supplies. Including a robot dog."

"My kind or your kind?" Dolly asks.

"My kind," Bits says. "I know this'll be hard for you to agree with, but if we get in there hard and fast and get it done before they really know what's going on, even if it is a trap, that's probably our best bet."

"So the robot dog is for...?" I start.

"I can use one to crash all of the internet connected devices in a radius. Which also means that we'll have a period of no contact, because even walkies would be too risky in this context."

"Oh yeah obviously," Dolly says, in a tone that says no, not obviously.

"If the freight elevator went to the roof, which it does, and we had access to a helicopter, we could just whisk it away," Bits says.

"Yeah, too bad I left all my helicopters at home," Dolly says.

"One of these times, we'll get you in one for a crucial part of the job, darling," I say, laying my hand on her wrist.

"Sure, sure, one day." The waitress walks past our table yet again, indicating we've more than overstayed our welcome, and then some.

"Let's adjourn to my hotel," Dolly says grandly.

"I can't believe we're doing this," Bits says. "I didn't think we should do a casino job to begin with, much less twice."

"It isn't *really* a casino job, darling," I say, and both of them just look at me.

Chapter Sixteen

Dolly is staying in a surprisingly nice hotel, given her predilection for what she refers to as 'no-tell motels' when we're in the States. It isn't a five star establishment by any means, but it is a perfectly respectable hotel with a restaurant and room service and a mini bar in the rooms. Also, she could put her shoes out to be shined, should she desire.

There is a little sitting area, and Bits sprawls on the couch while I arrange myself in an armchair and Dolly raids the mini-bar and drags over a straight backed chair from the desk that's in the bedroom.

"Okay, so faceless robot dog, no chopper, what're we doing for the dress-up portion of this, anything? Just civvies?"

"The jumpsuits weren't a terrible imposition," I say soothingly. "And you got to drive about the countryside with another gearhead."

"Sure I did. But is your pet designer gonna have the time to do something for you?"

"She isn't exactly my *pet*," I protest, laughing. "I bought one single item from her."

"Yeah but you're thinking about more. You always are."

"Like this planning session, for instance," Bits says helpfully.

"Wait, I know, you're just sad you missed Dolly dress up," she says, as she uses her forearm to twist the cap off her fresh bottle of cider. She's looking down as she says it, but I see the look on Bits's face and feel a rare twist of regret. "Sorry we didn't take the time to take any pictures, or at least I didn't, did—"

"No, I didn't take any pictures," Bits says, looking at me now, assessing what she thinks of the conversation about this that Dolly and I apparently had.

"That's a shame, darlings, truly, but I do understand," I say, almost automatically. "While dress up *would* be fun, if we're simply slipping up the freight elevator, I'm not sure it's necessary? Or I could come through the front and meet Dolly *at* the freight elevator?"

"Why would you do that?" Bits asks.

"Well dependin' on robot dog deployment, I'll need to know the coast is clear. Plus she's gotta break more hearts and maybe bet a stack of chips and win this time."

"Depending on robot dog deployment, Bristol won't be able to tell you if the coast is clear," Bits says patiently.

"Yeah you're right, we're complicating things. Let's just snag a truck or whatever and get over there."

"*Now?*" Bits says, staring at Dolly, looking at me as I sip the canned rosé from the mini bar.

"Perhaps Dolly is right, we are unnecessarily complicating matters and should just act."

"Just the three of us? For a casino?"

Dolly grins. "Well, as Bristol keeps sayin', it ain't *really* a casino job."

To say we're old hand at this is correct, but our excitement on the way to the casino is festive, electric. Reckless. We did all that preparation ahead of time, though, what more could we possibly need now for a grab, not even something so gauche as a smash and grab? First we take public transit, and then when we are on foot, Dolly locates a vehicle that she's certain the giraffe will fit in at the right angle, some model of station wagon.

"Too bad the active camo won't help us," Dolly says. "Unless you reverse engineered it, Bits? Built one we can use for something big as the giraffe?"

"I didn't, no," Bits mutters. She's going along with us, despite her misgiving, or because she thinks that without her, we shall fail tragically and utterly, which I suppose is a possibility but I feel unable to give it any worry. We shall succeed or we will not, we have done more dangerous things. Perhaps that's it; I don't believe in the *danger* of this.

Bits, of course, can imagine the danger for all of us and more, and Dolly thrives on it.

"Did they add extra surveillance?" I ask, so that Bits will talk to us more.

"Not that I can see," Bits says. "Which I don't want to trust, but I have to, right?"

"If Bitsy can't see it, it isn't there," Dolly agrees.

"I don't—"

"No, I agree, darling. If you can't see it, then it isn't the case. You absolutely cannot start doubting yourself at this late date."

Silence from the back seat, Bits checking and rechecking, I presume.

"Okay so here's the front door, Bristles, act normal, we'll be in touch." Dolly looks at me as I get out. "You bettin' again?"

I smile at her. "Mais oui. I must know." She laughs as I shut the door and walk inside.

The plan is simple as can be. I walk in, spend some time on the floor to make certain attention is away from the giraffe, notify Bits and Dolly of anything the surveillance cameras and such won't have informed Bits of. Dolly comes up the freight elevator and spirits the giraffe away, and I make my exit once she is clear and I'm certain nothing untoward is going to occur.

It is almost certainly unnecessary for me to be involved in this way. I was able to handle the statue myself in the first place, Dolly hardly needs my physical help. Bits has certainly gained access to every digital device at the location, but if she has concerns that they're doing things that she can't see, I'm more than happy to take this role.

I leave my coat on, simply go to get chips, the same amount as the other night. The men in the cage are not the same, and neither is the soccer game, the details all just different enough to prevent deja vu.

I trail about, watching and listening, but everything is sedate in the early evening on this weekday. The security guards are so easily spotted that I find myself looking about for the real guards, as though the obvious ones are decoys. What a funny thought to have, though it pays to trust one's instincts. //I believe everything is clear,// I say, ever so softly.

//Understood,// Dolly says.

I return to the same roulette table, where the dealer is different, and there are three bettors, two men and a woman. I wait until it is time to bet, and again put all of my chips on red 27. The dealer looks at that, and then at my face. "Rien ne va plus," he says a moment later.

//Bristol, he pressed a button,// Bits says in my ear. I hum an assent, softly enough that my cunning little microphone will pick it up but nobody else around the table.

The ball spins and so does the wheel, and they slow, and slow, and the ball clatters into a slot right as somebody, a man stops near me, a tasteful whiff of Bay Rum wafting to me. "Mademoiselle, you return," that tiresome man from the other night says.

"Bravo, mademoiselle," the dealer says, and very suddenly there are quite a lot of chips in front of me.

"I couldn't let my only roulette experience be a losing bet," I say, turning to the man. We should, perhaps, have realized he might have been casino staff, but I think his apparent intoxication is what discounted the very notion for me. Honestly, he was simply a pest to be gotten rid of. I smile, peering up into his face. "Perhaps you wouldn't mind helping mademoiselle cash in her chips? I've never done so before."

"It would be my pleasure," he says. He wants to be suspicious of me in some way, I think, but also cannot decide how. "Was this your plan? To return? You left so abruptly the other night, like Cinderella."

"Shoes intact, though," I say, and I can't help but laugh. He laughs too, and we both glance down at my shoes, which are unremarkable, comfortable, black leather pumps. "No, I didn't decide until I was out and about today that I would return."

"So your roulette career, it is finished?" he asks as we get to the cage.

"Well yes, I've had the low, and now the high. It's a game of chance; what more is left?"

"Nothing, I suppose," he says, laughing as we push my chips through to the employee, who looks at me, and looks at the man with me. "She put everything on one number."

"Congratulations, mademoiselle," the employee says.

"Merci," I say graciously. "And thank you for helping me. I suppose I could have found a little basket, like at the market?"

"And then I would have been deprived of the pleasure of your company," he says.

//Bristol, for somebody who doesn't like pets, you sure are good at pickin' up strays,// Dolly's voice says in my ear.

"And I yours," I say, smiling. The man in the cage goes to count my money, but Mr. Casino is still here next to me. "Shall we exchange names?"

"We should, but then we'll lose some of the magic," he says. He's laying it on thick, though not without charm. I'm certain that sort of line has melted many a heart.

I'm startled as I hear an unfamiliar voice on our network and it's only through all of my practice in front of a mirror that I'm certain my expression doesn't change.

"You can't come this way," a man says. Security, perhaps. Very close to Dolly, for me to hear him so clearly, that's unusual for her.

"I'm just doing what the instructions say, I'm not trying to give anybody a hard time," Dolly says, very much in an 'I don't make up the rules, I'm just doing my job' tone of voice.

Mr. Casino has something of a distracted look on *his* face, but then I'm being given quite a lot of cash. I cannot disentangle myself from this quickly enough to help Dolly, who I know can take care of herself, obviously, but we are responsible for each other, n'est-ce pas?

"Perhaps you'll require a market basket to leave with," he says finally, refocusing on me.

"And to think I left mine at home," I say. "I also don't have any little mice to draw a carriage for me."

"Such a shame."

Dolly comes back in, "Yeah that's fine, call them, I don't want to mess this whole thing up. It's fine, relax, I"ll stand right here and you can call them.......woah are you okay? Here sit down over here."

//He'll be okay,// Bits says. //I just made his pacemaker skip a few beats.//

//You can do that?// Dolly asks. //Like we joke about how you can do anything, but...//

//Not all pacemakers are online, but this one is. But also he just looked you right in the face. And so did Bristol's mark a couple days ago.//

//Just means it's another casino I can't bet at anymore. Let's get this show on the road.// The freight elevator dings; I think, I hope, that she is on her way *out*. //Hope you got your special lipstick with you, Bristles.//

"If you'll excuse me —" I start to say, and then my phone rings. "Oh!"

"Of course," he says, standing off.

I find my phone in my purse, confused about why Bits or Dolly might be *calling* me, but it's Suzette. She's gotten tired of

my not answering her messages, but we've just been so busy...
"Hello?"

"Bristol finally!" She says, and I can't tell if she's laughing or crying.

"Darling what is it? Are you all right?" Mr. Casino turns towards me at my tone, but remains at a distance.

"Yes! I think so! Nicolai proposed."

"He *did*?" Perhaps that's why he also called me, to ask advice for a ring. "What did you say? You accepted of course?"

"Of course! I'm thrilled but also I'm in a complete panic! I don't even speak Russian."

I can't help but laugh. "If that's all that's worrying you, then everything will be fine."

"You always say everything will be fine," she says.

"And you should believe it more often." I cover the mouthpiece a moment. "My friend, friends have just gotten engaged," I say.

"Oh indeed," he says

//Oh Nicky finally did it!// Dolly crows.

I can imagine the wince on Bits's face, but she takes a moment and then says, //Okay Bristol, Dolly is to the car, you can figure out your exit. Because that guard couldn't reach his boss, he approached Dolly on his own, but he isn't going to be out of it for much longer.//

"Suzette, darling, I do hate to let you go so soon and with all we need to talk about, but I am rather in the middle of something. I'll call you tomorrow?"

"Oh of course, I'm so sorry, I didn't think to ask."

"Don't you dare apologize to me for calling with news of your engagement!" Laughing, we hang up.

Mr. Casino looks bemused. "Since you've cashed out, and intend on leaving, shall I call mademoiselle a car?"

"That won't be necessary," I say with confidence, even though Bits and Dolly have gone silent in my ears.

"Then I must bid you adieu, there is something that requires my attention." He really is more charming than he seemed at first; he must have different personae when moving incognito on the casino floor. "Can I give you my card, at least?"

"Your card?" I repeat. "Well I suppose, yes."

"Thank you. I hope to see you again." He hands me what appears to be a business card, and then starts away in a walk that says it will become something more brisk once he is out of sight.

I also turn, and walk out the automatic doors, money crammed into my purse and my pockets. A car *is* there waiting, and I'm surprised when Will gets out and opens the door for me. "Bits said to go outside and get in the car, and when Bits tells me to do something, I do," he says, checking his mirrors and then pulling into traffic.

"But how..."

//It's got a self driving mode, so I just manipulated that,// Bits says in our ears.

//Is there anything Bits *can't* do,// Dolly says in proud admiration. I put my AR glasses on, look at the business card, front and back, to capture the information, then open the window a crack and let the wind snatch it from my fingers

//Windows,// Bits says, and then laughs in a way that suggests the rest of us don't quite get her joke.

Epilogue

Bits and I go to the airport with Dolly, giving her a reasonable amount of time to get through security for her flight, and perhaps even avail herself of one of the airport bars.

"Dolly, thank you ever so much for coming to do this with us," I say, both not everything that I want to say and also enough that she understands me.

"I could hardly miss the party," she says, grinning. "A casino —"

"It was *not*—"

"We get it," Bits says, with her anxious 'eyes and ears are everywhere' expression. "But yeah, I agree. Thank you Dolly."

"Hong Kong is terribly far away," I say after a pause.

"Sure, but you'll see me at Nicolai's wedding. And you'll only stay put here for so long, even if it *is* Paris."

"You're right, of course," I say with a sigh. She surprises me, us, by giving each of us a firm hug.

"See you when I see you," she says in my ear, and then she's away and walking through the airport to the first security checkpoint.

"I'm glad you got to talk," Bits says, watching me and not Dolly.

"I am too," I say, watching Dolly cut through the crowd a moment before turning away. "And that wasn't so bad, now was it?"

"Better than expected," she agrees. "Nobody ever even took a shot."

About the Author

Jennifer R. Donohue grew up at the Jersey Shore and now lives in central New York with her husband and their Doberman. She works at her local public library where she also facilitates a writing workshop. Her work has appeared in *Apex Magazine*, *Escape Pod*, *Fantasy*, *The Deadlands Fusion Fragment*, and elsewhere. Her debut novel, Exit Ghost, is available now. You can find her Bluesky @AuthorizedMusings.bsky.social, and you can subscribe to her Patreon for a new short story every month: https://www.patreon.com/JenniferRDonohue

Further work by Jennifer R. Donohue
Exit Ghost
The Drowned Heir
Between the Blood and the Sun
The Learn to Howl Trilogy
Learn to Howl
Baying the Moon
The Company of Wolves
Other books in the Run With the Hunted series
Run With the Hunted
Run With the Hunted 2: Ctrl Alt Delete
Run With the Hunted 3: Standard Operating Procedure
Run With the Hunted 4: VIP
Run With the Hunted 5: Insert Coin to Play
Run With the Hunted 6: Burned Asset